More acclaim for *The*

"A fun and funny novel."   —*The New York Sun*

"The only problem with *The Yoga Mamas* is that it's extremely difficult to put down. . . . For most readers, a peek into the lives—and lofts—of this wealthy and stylish group is made more fun by the down-to-earth ballast of the protagonist, Laura. . . . It all leads to a sweet and deeply satisfying ending."   —*New York Family*

"[*The Yoga Mamas*] capture[s] the walking dilemma that is the new mother: navigating playground politics, new friendships, sleepless nights, and saying good-bye to the old life while free-falling into an exciting (and sometimes terrifying) new world. Kick off your shoes, pour a cool drink, and enjoy."   —UrbanBaby.com

"From making status symbols out of strollers to flaunting posh gifts with exorbitant price tags and coping with nursery school waiting list woes, *The Yoga Mamas* is a delightful glimpse at new motherhood among five pregnant urban women . . . [a] funny account of true friendship."   —SavvyMummy.com

"You have to read this book . . . you'll laugh, you'll cry . . . you'll want to read it again!"   TheDailyStroll.com

"Here's a yoga-themed novel just for fun. Replace the Manolo Blahniks with high-end strollers and the Cosmos with grilled tofu sandwiches, and you've got the ultimate in chick lit for mothers and mothers-to-be. Set around SoHo's prenatal yoga scene, this gossipy novel offers up a saucy ride and a twist to rival a yogini's spine."   —*Today's Parent*

Berkley Books by Katherine Stewart

THE YOGA MAMAS
CLASS MOTHERS

CLASS MOTHERS

Katherine Stewart

BERKLEY BOOKS, NEW YORK

THE BERKLEY PUBLISHING GROUP
Published by the Penguin Group
Penguin Group (USA) Inc.
375 Hudson Street, New York, New York 10014, USA
Penguin Group (Canada), 90 Eglinton Avenue East, Suite 700, Toronto, Ontario M4P 2Y3, Canada
(a division of Pearson Penguin Canada Inc.)
Penguin Books Ltd., 80 Strand, London WC2R 0RL, England
Penguin Group Ireland, 25 St. Stephen's Green, Dublin 2, Ireland (a division of Penguin Books Ltd.)
Penguin Group (Australia), 250 Camberwell Road, Camberwell, Victoria 3124, Australia
(a division of Pearson Australia Group Pty. Ltd.)
Penguin Books India Pvt. Ltd., 11 Community Centre, Panchsheel Park, New Delhi—110 017, India
Penguin Group (NZ), Cnr. Airborne and Rosedale Roads, Albany, Auckland 1310, New Zealand
(a division of Pearson New Zealand Ltd.)
Penguin Books (South Africa) (Pty.) Ltd., 24 Sturdee Avenue, Rosebank, Johannesburg 2196, South Africa

Penguin Books Ltd., Registered Offices: 80 Strand, London WC2R 0RL, England

This book is an original publication of The Berkley Publishing Group.

This is a work of fiction. Names, characters, places, and incidents either are the product of the author's imagination or are used fictitiously, and any resemblance to actual persons, living or dead, business establishments, events, locales is entirely coincidental. The publisher does not have any control over and does not assume any responsibility for author or third-party websites or their content.

CLASS MOTHERS

First edition: July 2006

Berkley trade paperback ISBN: 0-425-20792-7

An application to register this book for cataloging has been submitted to the Library of Congress.

PRINTED IN THE UNITED STATES OF AMERICA

10 9 8 7 6 5 4 3 2 1

Acknowledgments

I would like to thank my superb editor, Kate Seaver, and my wonderful agent, Andrew Stuart. A special thanks to Mim Udovitch. I am also grateful to Sally Ross, Rebecca van de Sande, Suzanne Seggerman, Alex King, Liz Tedford, and above all, my patient and loving husband.

Chapter 1

One, two,
Buckle my shoe

"Children's table-and-chairs set, hand-painted in organic pigments by Miss Caspar's four-year-olds class. Estimated value: five thousand dollars . . .

"One-year membership at the Bloom Club and Spa, including four pedicures, three blowouts, two Frequent-Flier Body Scrubs featuring specially harvested salts from each of the seven seas, and one consultation with a life coach. Estimated value: seven thousand five hundred dollars . . .

"Walk-on role in *Sex and the City: The Movie*. Involves a nonspeaking part in a bar scene. Estimated value: fifteen thousand dollars . . .

"Winter week for two at Iguana Cay, a private island compound in the Turks and Caicos. Includes private jet transport, personal chef and butler, spa, tennis and parasailing, plus four beach ensembles supplied courtesy of Calypso . . ."

Sunny, the cheerful school director, rolled her tongue around the complementary Calypso ensembles as if they were a mouthful of gummy bears.

"Estimated value: . . . thirty thousand dollars!"

She shook her copper-colored hair in wonder and spread a hearty laugh around the room. The four of us chuckled obediently.

"Eve and Jeffrey were so generous to donate the use of their private vacation home to the school auction," Bronwyn said breathlessly, a wide smile breaking across her high-cheekboned face, softening her pale, almost glacial beauty. Tiny crow's-feet formed at the corners of her honey-colored eyes. She shook her hair, which hung in silky sheets to the middle of her back, with the confidence of the classic American blonde and brushed some imaginary lint off her white cashmere turtleneck. Bronwyn was the chairwoman of the annual fund-raising auction committee and the unofficial queen bee of the Metropolitan Preschool parent body—rich, thin, beautiful, and endlessly dedicated.

"The Caribbean is *so* crowded these days," Dominique said less enthusiastically in her light French accent. "In Barbados, everyone used to know everyone. Now there is a Banana Republic on the *Rue Maritime*."

If Bronwyn was the perfect American blonde, then Dominique was the epitome of the sulky yet sensual Frenchwoman. Unlikely to be in regular contact in any other context, Metropolitan Preschool had made them strange bedfellows. Dominique's moody gray eyes sparkled behind heavy lashings of mascara and dark liner flicked at the corners. She had bronzed skin that spoke of a Gallic disregard for UV warnings. Dirty blond locks escaped from an unruly chignon. As always, she had styled herself like a gypsy on a platinum-card budget. She wore a hand-tooled leather belt over an embroidered tunic and a tangle of bulky turquoise and hammered gold necklaces.

"Have we checked the pricing on this?" said Kim in clipped tones. "Thirty K sounds low to me." She had a strangely deliberate way of pronouncing her vowels. I couldn't tell if it was the remnant of an accent or just a personal quirk. Her solid frame and chin-length dark hair remained fixed in place, aiming straight at Sunny. Her features were austere and angular, though not without a certain elegance. She was on the auction committee, but with her reserved, no-nonsense attitude, somehow she was not of it. I guessed that she was of Korean descent.

With nothing immediate to contribute, I tried picturing Richard and me on holiday at Jeffrey and Eve's Iguana Cay estate, but then I realized that the week of pleasure would leave us in credit-card hell for the rest of our lives. *Besides,* I thought, looking around my imaginary Caribbean island, *where would we hide Anna?* "It sounds like a great offer," I said, thinking aloud. "But why is it an offer for *two*? Shouldn't we include the whole family?"

Dominique rolled her eyes to the heavens. Kim snorted audibly. Bronwyn shot me a concerned look, as if to say, *After all the lessons I've given you?*

Kim opened her mouth into a snarl and looked like she was about to say something, but Bronwyn swiftly cut her off. "It'll be great with the tropics theme, Laura, won't it?"

"Oh, yes," I chirped, happy to change the subject. "Maybe we could do something with the island idea. . . ."

Somehow, by something close to sheer random chance, I had become Metropolitan's tropical authority. This was, in fact, the only reason I was on the school's auction committee at all. In New York City, the world capital of communications, if you don't have money, you can always earn your place at the table with information. As it happened, the advertising agency I worked for as a freelance consultant had recently taken on a number of clients in the Caribbean tourist industry, and I had become the de facto set designer for some of their shoots. I knew where to buy fake palm trees and coconuts, I had the number for a great steel drum trio, and I could mix the perfect mojito. At one point in the previous year I'd even created an artificial island, which pleased the client so much, I'd been given a bonus. When I mentioned my work to Sunny, she put me directly in touch with Bronwyn, who enthusiastically adopted me as her protégée on the auction committee, despite the disparity in our tax brackets.

"The island idea, yes, but how?" Bronwyn said. "Maybe bring in an aquarium with tropical fish?"

"I know," I said, "we could create a little island! With sand!"

"Yes!" Bronwyn nodded vigorously. "We could truck in some sand and put in a pool!"

"*Mais, c'est fantastique!*" Dominique responded, her sensual languor turning to animation. "We could have little waves in the pool! We could put in real fish! We could have those charming fishing boats, and get some of those gorgeous young Jamaican men to row them. Without their shirts, of course . . ."

"You could organize that, Laura, couldn't you?"

I laughed in acknowledgment. We might want to ditch some of Dominique's wilder ideas, but I knew I could re-create an island environment.

"We haven't got time for this!" Kim interjected in her businesslike staccato. "I need to get back to the office by five. Let's focus on the bottom line! I think we can ask thirty-five K for the Iguana Cay place."

"Well, I——" Bronwyn began to say, somewhat defensively. She had done almost all the work in compiling the auction catalog.

"Wonderful!" Sunny said, clearly accustomed to putting out the brush fires of parental politics. She jotted down the new number. "Let's talk about the decorations at our next meeting, shall we?" Then she glanced at Bronwyn and raised a knowing eyebrow. When it came to sending subliminal emotional cues, Sunny had skills that cult leaders might envy, and her glance managed to convey the message: *Relax, you've done good work—and, yes, Kim is pretty tense.* Bronwyn's cheeks dimpled and she flashed Sunny a look of thanks. Kim remained as guarded as always. Dominique blew on a stray lock, doing nothing to disguise her boredom now that our Caribbean theme park had been momentarily put on hold.

Once upon a time, the Metropolitan Preschool had been a utopian collective stranded among the derelict warehouses of lower Manhattan, and Sunny had been a ponytailed crusader for "progressive education." An old Polaroid photograph hanging near the entrance showed Sunny in a smock and sandals, her face beaming with idealistic zeal from behind an armful of tots in tie-dyed T-shirts. I could still see something of that bright-eyed young woman in the cheerful headmistress in front of me. Her hippie garb had ceded to a modest rust-colored suit, and her casual locks had been bobbed to the chin. But she still wore a wide, welcoming smile. Her slightly crooked posture, the legacy of a childhood battle with polio, endeared her to anyone who heard the story and gave her the noble air of a survivor. An enormous opal pendant on a thick gold chain glinted with kaleidoscopic optimism on her generous bosom.

In the past thirty years, as TriBeCa evolved into "Triburbia," a desirable place for the princes of Wall Street to park their pampered families, Sunny had transformed the school along with it. The old, cast-iron façade now had storefront windows on the classrooms overlooking the street. From the opposite sidewalk, it could easily be confused with one of the neighborhood's high-end boutiques, or perhaps an art gallery with an unusual exhibit. But in the anxious eyes of New York parents, a spot in one of those classrooms glistened as brightly and desirably as the Nobel Prize. Movie stars and television newscasters duked it out with the merely rich to secure admission for their offspring. Society matrons who bowed to no one shuffled and scraped, manipulating every variable within their manicured reach. One young mother reportedly moved across town to improve her tot's chances. "There were too many applicants in our old building," she said. Others gleefully confided the boldface names from whom they had managed to secure letters of recommendation: Rudy Giuliani, Martha Stewart, Christo. Through it all, Sunny, the ex–flower child, had blossomed into the grande dame of the city's educational aristocracy. "Forget Anna Wintour," Bronwyn had confided to me. "The most powerful woman in New York City is Sunny. Period."

Sunny clasped her hands and smiled at us again. "Ladies, I am truly impressed by all your hard work! Thanks to your efforts, the scholarship program will prosper."

Sunny and the other women were polite enough not to look in my direction, but they all knew that in a sense they were talking about me. My daughter, Anna, had been awarded Metropolitan's first Forsythe Scholarship, named in honor of the munificent Eve and Jeffrey Forsythe, of Iguana Cay auction fame.

I hadn't counted on Anna winning the scholarship. In fact, we hadn't even applied. When Anna was younger, I had vaguely envisioned sending her to some kind of local playgroup. I owed her presence at Metropolitan to my well-connected friend from prenatal yoga, Susan Fielding. Through a series of events too complicated to recount, I had helped Susan discover and then cope with the truth about her husband, Harcourt, whose misdeeds ranged from philandering to embezzling to tampering with the ladies on the board of Metropolitan. The scholarship was my reward.

It wasn't the standard way to secure a child's educational future, but truth be told, I was more grateful now than I could have imagined being before I became a parent. Motherhood, I had discovered, wasn't as simple as the television commercials I worked on made it look. Sometimes I felt as though I was pushing grains of sand from one pile to another, only to have them blow back together every night. The struggle was punctuated by the periodic demands of an employer who didn't want to hear about a sick child or leaky ceiling.

In the midst of this chaos, finding a preschool for Anna loomed like a rarified form of torture. Aside from the fact that most of the preschools were extraordinarily expensive, they also seemed so bizarrely selective. In some schools, as few as one in forty applicants was accepted. And the process would have included multiple interviews with Anna. I hated the idea of throwing my child into the rat race at such a ridiculously young age. But I also recoiled at the thought that my daughter wouldn't benefit from the advantages offered to the children of more privileged mothers.

Life in the playgrounds of lower Manhattan only made matters worse. There, I'd invariably see one or two mommies determined to lure others into asking them where they sent their offspring to preschool. Then they'd pounce. They'd watch with undisguised glee as the name of this or that prestigious school flattened out their victims like a blast from a Super Soaker. It reminded me of a friend who had attended a certain college in Boston, who occasionally allowed herself to revel in the effects of what she called the "H-bomb." But in the parks of lower Manhattan, Harvard degrees were as common as cigarette butts. You needed the M-bomb if you really wanted to do some damage.

At home, Richard and I agreed that the whole thing was rather distasteful. "It's just preschool!" he'd say to anybody who would listen. "No matter where you send them, they still come home with the same painted macaroni!"

That was Richard. He was New York University's resident expert on seventeenth-century Holland, and often he saw things in the clean lines of a flat Dutch landscape of windmills and canals. Sometimes I wasn't so sure. I wondered if my husband had lost track of the fact that we lived in twenty-first-century Manhattan.

Sunny returned to the list of auction goodies. There were tickets to *Vanity Fair*'s A-list Oscars party, weekends at a range of country homes, a chance to announce the weather on a local news channel, and a pair of leopard-print sofas. There were even a few items that fell within my freelancer's budget: a children's outfit from Bu and the Duck; a kids' haircut at Whipper Snippers; a large pie with your choice of toppings and a round of sodas at Bazzini on Hudson Street.

Autumn sunlight filtered in through south-facing windows and glinted off the network of exposed ducts and sprinkler systems running beneath the high tin ceiling. The Metropolitan Preschool occupied the first two floors of a converted textile factory. A maze of irregular partitions carved the space into classrooms. Straining, I could hear the distant sounds of children at play.

"Three, four, shut the door!" one of the kids was yelling as the others squealed and giggled. Anna and the offspring of the three other mothers were staying after school in the care of Tori, Anna's teacher. Tori couldn't have been older than twenty-three or twenty-four, and she seemed a little unsure of herself in the classroom. But I told myself that she made up for her lack of experience with her enthusiasm for her young charges. To occupy the kids during the auction committee meeting, she had devised a "science project" that involved the kids inspecting the class pet, a white hamster named Snowflake.

"Blueblerries! Blueblerries! Blueblerries for Snowflake!"

That, of course, was Anna. "Blueblerries" was one of her several mispronunciations, such as "eggs-stink," "ugguley," and even "You Nork," which I found too cute to correct. Ever since her third birthday, when I'd bought her the classic children's book *Blueberries for Sal,* she'd enjoyed pretending to feed blueberries and milk to her stuffed animals at home. But today she could play the game with a real live hamster.

Sunny continued to read from the hypnotic list of auction goodies. "Oh, I just *love* this one!" she said, adjusting her glasses and leaning in close to the sheet of paper. "A film of the auction itself, produced and directed by our very own Quentin—" She broke off and looked up. "That's Foxxy's daddy to us."

All of a sudden, I heard the all-too-familiar screeches of my daughter throwing an unholy tantrum. I closed my eyes and willed the noise to stop. This was the new side of Anna. As a two-year-old, Anna had been cheerful and obedient, the model of a loving and inquisitive toddler. When I thought back on those early days of new motherhood, I remembered a dreamy wonderworld as Anna learned new ways to express humor, curiosity, and affection. When other mothers complained about "the terrible twos," I secretly congratulated myself for having been blessed with the sweetest daughter alive.

But when Anna turned three, my smug attitude boomeranged, slapping me senseless. She had taken a running leap into the "trysome threes," as they say in some of the parenting books.

It started with the word *no*, which Anna emphatically uttered whenever I asked, suggested, or ordered her to do anything, particularly pertaining to her own safety. Then she moved on to food—which she treated as material for wall decoration. During her many public tantrums, usually timed to ensure maximum embarrassment and discomfort for Mommy, I sometimes felt a guilty sympathy for those parents who ended up spanking their kids—though I had vowed never to raise a hand against my precious little devil.

"She was born under Mercury," my old friend Susan explained, "so she has a lot of fire in her."

"She's been eating too much sugar," Richard claimed.

"She's spoiled," my mom said flatly.

Eventually, Richard and I had put our spawn in front of a child psychologist. "We don't believe in the devil," Richard told him, "but we are willing to consider exorcism."

The therapist observed us at play from behind a one-way mirror, scheduled a separate meeting at which he mumbled something about "testing boundaries," then sent us a bill that was roughly equivalent to a month's rent. We never went back.

"This is fabulous work! Fabulous!" Sunny concluded, pretending not to hear my daughter's demented shrieks. I cringed, but, fortunately, Anna seemed to have finally received my urgent telepathic commands and was starting to quiet down.

Just then I heard a muffled buzzing sound. Sunny pulled a small telephone out of her jacket pocket. "Ladies, I do apologize," she announced, flipping open the cover to read a text message. "I have to excuse myself for just a minute. Back in three ticks!"

The moment Sunny stepped out the door, Bronwyn turned to us with a conspiratorial smile on her face. "Hey, guys, I just got some interesting information," she whispered. Bronwyn always had interesting information. She was like a one-woman CIA in the world of Manhattan schools—she knew who was applying where, who was getting in, and which strings they pulled to get there. "I've heard that Holyfield is going to be really tight this year because of a high number of siblings."

Somehow, most conversations among Metropolitan mothers came around to the subject of admissions to Holyfield, New York's most prestigious kindergarten and grade school, or "ongoing school" in the private-school lingo. Parents gave any number of reasons for wanting to get their children into Metropolitan. They could boast of the curriculum based on a cutting-edge educational philosophy. They could tout the favorable student/teacher ratios. Or they could marvel at the elaborate art projects their children brought home, such as the "Greek myth masks," which I was pretty certain had in fact been assembled by Anna's teachers. But the real attraction of Metropolitan was that it vastly improved one's chances of getting into Holyfield Academy. In New York society, the only acceptable comeback to "We've just closed on a classic six with a view of Central Park" is "My daughter will be graduating from Holyfield."

Of course, like all such schools, Holyfield had a policy of making room for siblings. The "sibling issue" in particular filled parents of only children—such as me—with a quiet sense of moral outrage. In my more paranoid moments it seemed that parents whose firstborn got accepted at the most desirable preschools then had extra kids, just to hog the available spots. Family size had become a new status symbol in Manhattan, the quickest way to signal more square footage, more nannies, more tuition bills—in short, more money and power. "Four is the new three," I had heard more than one playground mother chirp.

"Incredible!" said Dominique, at the mention of Holyfield. "Did you know that at Holyfield, Uma Thurman conducts the children's drama productions!"

Dominique still had the accoutrements of her years as a foreign film star: the confidence bordering on insouciance, the wardrobe spiced with haute couture, and the pied-à-terre on the Côte d'Azur. As far as I knew, she hadn't made a movie since her child was born. But when she walked into a room, people still whispered and stared.

"And Richard Gere organized a school audience with the Dalai Lama." Bronwyn nodded appreciatively. "His twins go there, you know. . . ."

Kim wrinkled her nose. "The important thing is that sixty-three percent of Holyfield graduates are admitted to the Ivy League school *of their choice*," she announced. Kim was a busy executive—a hedge fund manager, as she reminded everyone at every opportunity. With her businesslike wardrobe and brusque manners, she seemed as intimidating to me as the tinted limousines that whizzed by the sidewalks outside my apartment block and splashed water on my shoes.

"But I cannot believe the school is perfect," Dominique said to Bronwyn, ignoring Kim. "At a cocktail party, I met this woman who says that there is a real problem with drugs in the middle school."

"She's just saying that because she doesn't want you to apply,"

Bronwyn replied, raising her eyebrows sympathetically. "The same thing happens on UrbanBaby.com. Women spread nasty rumors about a particular school whenever they are trying to shrink the applicant pool."

I had heard many similar stories of such cutthroat behavior. Moms were often caught misleading fellow parents about admissions deadlines. Others claimed to have been blackballed from various private schools as retribution for the most minor social transgressions. If your child was in the market for schools, all of your new-mommy friendships suddenly turned into rivalries.

I resolved to quash any fantasies I might have entertained of securing yet another scholarship for Anna.

"Well, if Holyfield doesn't work out, we're zoned for some pretty good public schools," I said, thinking aloud.

Bronwyn looked at me with genuine concern. In her mind, public schools occupied the same space as juvenile detention centers.

Then her face brightened at a new thought. "Why don't you join Park Avenue Presbyterian?" she said to me. "They've got a great school. We go every Sunday, just in case Holyfield doesn't work out."

"But I thought you were Catholic. . . ." Dominique started.

Kim cut her off. "Well, maybe there are scholarships for the disadvantaged at Holyfield," she said bluntly. My mouth dropped inadvertently into fly-catching position. So I was . . . *disadvantaged*? Bronwyn looked appalled. Even Dominique arched a well-groomed eyebrow.

Just then, Sunny appeared at the door to the room. She seemed to have picked up the gist of our conversation. "Holyfield?" She smiled. "I'm going to share something with you ladies. You deserve to be the first to know."

The members of the Metropolitan auction committee leaned forward ever so slightly in their chairs. Kim pursed her lips. Bronwyn furled her brow. Another lock fell from Dominique's chignon.

"Thanks to Eve and Jeffrey Forsythe, who understand as well as anyone what we are trying to achieve here at Metropolitan, my colleagues have allowed me two places on the early-admissions roster at Holyfield . . ."

The early-admissions roster, of course, was simply a set of places to be filled at the discretion of Sunny and a handful of people like her.

"And I believe there may even be a scholarship still available," she added, smiling warmly at me.

I smiled back with undisguised gratitude. Out of the corner of my eye, I could see the other women exchanging wary glances. The naked truth was that as members of the auction committee, we stood the best chance of winning Sunny's favor and securing the coveted spots at Holyfield. But there were four of us. And only two places. We all did the math silently. At least two of us weren't going to make it.

"I will let you get on with your work," Sunny said, stepping back out the door. "Let me just go check on our pupils!"

Kim, Dominique, Bronwyn, and I looked at each other in silence for a moment.

"It is good news, no?" Dominique said.

"Yes, we can do it," Bronwyn said. She seemed to believe that if we all tried hard enough, we could defy the math and prove that one plus one equals four.

Kim pulled out a cell phone and pretended to look for messages. No getting around the math for her.

While we chatted idly, the activity in the children's room increased once again. I heard my devil-child raise her voice. Just as the noise reached a crescendo, we could hear Sunny's voice, faint but distinct: "Oh dear! Oh *dear!*"

"I'm sorry . . . I didn't see . . ." we heard Tori say.

We exchanged urgent glances. Something was very wrong. We shot up out of our chairs in unison and headed for the kids.

We bumped into Sunny at the doorway to the classroom. She was cradling a bundle of paper towels in her arms. She looked startled to see us.

"What is it?" Bronwyn demanded.

Sunny hesitated, looking flustered, and shook her head. She was breathing too rapidly, and seemed at a loss for words.

"What?" Kim said anxiously.

"I'm going to have to ask you all to maintain absolute discretion," Sunny said shakily, stepping outside the room and collecting herself. "I needn't remind you just how damaging this kind of . . . rumor . . . can be to a child's permanent record."

We looked at each other nervously, the word *Holyfield* occupying the entirety of our collective consciousness.

"I will assign a preceptor to investigate. We don't know who is responsible yet." "Preceptor" was Metropolitan's euphemism for "child psychologist."

Sunny paused.

We leaned forward.

She gingerly lifted open the bundle of paper towels, tilting it so the children could not see and allowing us a glimpse of its horrifying contents. I saw the inert body, its head twisted in an unnatural direction. As we stood back, aghast, Sunny eyed each of us in turn and whispered with a shudder, "Snowflake has been . . . murdered!"

Chapter 2

Along came a spider
Who sat down beside her . . .

The Rigatoni Factory Theater inhabited an old, redbrick warehouse on one of the narrow streets north of City Hall. In an earlier decade it had been the boozy haunting ground of Beat poets and the bohemian overflow from Greenwich Village. More recently, it had become a venue for children's theater productions and the odd chamber music ensemble. Today it was to be given over to a birthday party.

As I approached the entrance on a crisp fall afternoon, pushing Anna in the stroller with one hand, I fingered the invitation with the other. The crisp paper rustled expensively. It was in three different shades of pink, made of three different paper stocks, rough-cut at the edges, and tied together with a bow of hand-dyed raffia. It was more heavily designed than any wedding invitation I'd ever received—or sent out. In gold letters it recorded a line from Shakespeare about the innocence of youth and then requested its bearer's presence "onstage" for a birthday party in honor of Serena, who would be turning four.

Taking a cue from the invitation, I had dressed Anna in her best party dress and a pair of sparkly pink shoes to match. "Come on, Sweet Pea, let's show them how fancy you look!" I coaxed my daughter out of the stroller.

"Okay, Mommy," she replied happily, and toddled ahead of me into the small amphitheater. Immediately we ran into a wall of sound—the familiar cries of dozens of children making merry. "Mommy, look!" Anna pointed in wonder at a juggler onstage. I recognized some of the other kids from Anna's class chasing each other up and down the aisles while their parents and caregivers attempted to carry on adult conversations. To my dismay, the kids weren't the only ones wearing their party best; most of the mothers were wearing stylish skirts and ladylike heels. With my sneakers and oversized sweater, I blended in with the nannies, who were about as numerous as the moms.

I reached in the back of the stroller for the birthday gift I'd picked up on the way down—a store-wrapped copy of *Make Way for Ducklings,* one of my own favorite books as a child and a staple of Anna's bedtime library. Before I could put it down, a garishly outfitted clown assaulted us. He knelt next to Anna and thrust into her hands a glittery pink bag in the shape of a high-heeled shoe. It was the "girls" welcome gift; I'd already noticed a few of the boys carrying around red bags in the shape of trains. Anna opened the bag eagerly. It was stuffed with goodies: candy, toy dinosaurs, crayons, a picture frame, sequined and feathered sunglasses, and a set of toddler-sized nailpolishes in pastel shades.

Anna plopped down on the floor and began to smear her tiny fingers with lavender goo. I glanced at the refreshment tables. Champagne bottles jostled with quart-sized containers of fresh OJ from Dean & Deluca. There were panini and truffled risotto hors d'oeuvres for the adults and mini wedges of pizza for the kids. On a shelf carefully placed out of reach of tiny hands were cookies, cupcakes, and other colorful sweets. Flower arrangements in various shades of pink graced the tables, and pearlized orange balloons bobbed up against the ceiling.

I made my way to the table set aside for Serena's gifts. It was stacked high with dozens of bulky boxes bearing discreet labels from FAO Schwarz, Best & Co., and Bergdorf Goodman, each one professionally beribboned. At the side of the table was parked a pink-and-purple go-cart, complete with a toddler-size Barbie doll in the driver's seat. It had absentee-father guilt written all over it.

I realized that I had vastly underestimated the amount of money the parents of Metropolitan were inclined to spend on birthday gifts for one another's children. As I clutched my own modest offering, Kim's words about Anna's "disadvantaged" background echoed through my head. I couldn't have found a gift that said "scholarship mom" more loudly if I'd tried.

All of a sudden, I had a crazy thought. *Should I?* I glanced around quickly. No one was watching. *Why not!* I removed the identifying card off my gift, slipped it into the pile, and walked away quickly.

"Hi, I'm Serena's mom!"

I was suddenly face-to-face with a wiry brunette dressed in something like a fairy godmother costume. Her daughter, Serena, was at her side, fidgeting uncomfortably in her pink leotard, which was at least one size too small. Maribou-trimmed angel wings sprouted from her back. She tugged at her mom's filmy dress and pointed up to the tantalizing shelf of cookies and other goodies.

"Stop it, Serena!" her mom said, looking down at her with irritation. "How many times do I have to tell you? Do you want to be fat like your daddy? Fairy princesses are supposed to be light on their feet!"

She turned up to me with a bright smile.

"Serena's been taking Anastasia's ballet class for almost a year now," she said expansively. "We've been rehearsing her birthday solo all summer!"

I had once thought that getting into Metropolitan would be enough to resolve all possible concerns about one's child's future, but I was wrong, dead wrong. All of the kids, I had learned by now, were signed up for a range of extracurricular activities. Anastasia's ballet classes, as I had by now heard many times, were almost as difficult to get into as Metropolitan itself.

Serena tugged on her mother's fairy cape, but only halfheartedly. She was a big-boned girl with soft, rounded features. She had her mother's dark hair, but otherwise it was obvious that the father, who was nowhere to be seen, had cleaned up in the genetic sweepstakes.

"Oh, that's our cue!" Serena's mother exclaimed as the lights began to dim in the auditorium. A drumroll sounded across the stage, and mother and daughter raced behind the curtains.

While the pair lit up the stage with a rendition of "Sugarplum Fairies," Bronwyn's son, Harrison, a towheaded kid with big, chubby cheeks, ambled up to us with a mischievous expression and thrust his gift bag out front. He and Anna, whose dress was by now smeared with purple lacquer, immediately began peering into each other's goody bags. Bronwyn had told me she would be arriving late, and she had apparently sent Harrison ahead with his nanny, Bernadette. I looked around for Bernadette and finally spied her in the back row of the theater, deep in conversation with another nanny. The other nanny absentmindedly glanced at her own charge, a tall boy about Anna's age who was off on his own a few feet away from her. I recognized the reddish hair and large, serious, almond-shaped eyes: It was Kim's son, Jake.

I glanced between Jake and Harrison. Was one of them a hamster killer? I couldn't wash my mind of the picture of poor Snowflake, her neck twisted, her eyes unblinking. I scrutinized each kid carefully. I had to admit, they looked like ordinary little boys amusing themselves in ordinary ways. But why was Jake playing by himself like that? Was there something just a little manic in Harrison's expression?

I reached for Anna and drew her close. I'd spent the previous evening quietly probing her about the events of yesterday afternoon at Metropolitan. Questioning a three-year-old, of course, is a hit-or-miss affair—like most kids her age, Anna would often simply ignore my questions. But I'd also listened in on the stream of consciousness that she regularly offered to any and all within hearing range. I was convinced that she was innocent of any wrongdoing. In fact, she didn't seem to know that Snowflake had been murdered.

Anna, who had been watching Harrison silently, suddenly broke through my thoughts with her high-pitched squeals. She was holding an odd, somewhat pointy, sparkly object aloft.

"The pointy-point is *mine!*" she shrieked.

I realized that it was a piece of the glittery sunglasses that had originated in her goody bag.

"The pointy-point is *mine!*" Harrison shot back. He lunged for the disputed object, for some reason more valuable now that it was garbage rather than a recognizable item of any obvious utility, taking Anna down to the ground. The pair promptly descended into a life-or-death struggle, their cries reaching fever pitch.

"Kids!" I said, hastily stepping in the middle of it. "You have to share the pointy-point!" Then, reminding myself that "sharing" was not an appealing concept to three-year-olds, I began working on convincing Harrison that the miniature train from his own gift bag was much more fun. Since there are at least some ways in which a three-year-old is no match for an adult, in a minute or so, the two reverted to a state of peace, smiling and playing with each other as though nothing had happened.

At that moment, Bronwyn breezed into the room clutching a large box from Barneys.

"Just look at my sweetie boy!" she said with undisguised motherly pride. "He is so gentle," she added, looking at me meaningfully. "He's the kind of kid who would never hurt anyone or anything. . . . Thanks so much for watching over him. Here, I'll get Bernadette to take over so we can chat." She waved at her nanny, and we retreated to a quiet pair of seats in the back row of the auditorium.

"Bernadette is great," she whispered to me. "That's Betty she was talking to. They're both from Martinique. Betty works for Kim." She grimaced for an instant.

Our eyes fell on Jake, who was still sitting by himself and conducting odd chemistry experiments with cookies and juice.

"So what did you think of Jake's little performance yesterday?" Bronwyn whispered to me suddenly.

I looked at her with surprise. "Are you sure it was him?"

"Please!" she said, widening her eyes. "Everybody knows Jake has issues."

"How do you know?"

Bronwyn nodded furtively toward the nannies. "Jake was rejected from just about every preschool in the city. It's a developmental thing. They think maybe it's a mild form of autism. It's all very private, of course. No one is supposed to know."

"So how did he get into Metropolitan?" I asked.

"Kim is a hedge fund manager. She's probably got a lot to offer, if you know what I mean. Of course, she's also had to keep pulling the wool over people's eyes. Did you see how shocked Sunny looked? I think she was p.r.e.t.t.y. surprised. God, poor Snowflake."

Bronwyn paused again, allowing it all to sink in.

"Well," I said at last. "We'd better keep him away from our pets!"

Bronwyn frowned. "Yeah. But it could be more serious than that. He has a problem that needs to be acknowledged. And addressed."

As Bronwyn and I moved on to less loaded topics, the conversation grew more open. Originally, I had been Bronwyn's charity project, but more and more I was getting the feeling that in her own reserved way, she needed someone to talk to, perhaps someone who wasn't a part of her world. She told me about her move several years earlier from the Upper West Side to TriBeCa. I told her about the friends I'd made in prenatal yoga. We laughed about the trials and tribulations of urban parenting.

"It's all a bit much, isn't it?" Bronwyn said, rolling her eyes around the extravagant birthday party scene. "I mean, have you checked out the goody bags?"

I smiled.

"Of course, I have to admit, it reminds me of Harrison's first birthday." She shook her head self-deprecatingly. "I got so carried away planning it that Lloyd started calling me Martha-Mommy."

"I know what you mean," I said, thinking back on Anna's one-year-birthday cake, which I had special-ordered weeks in advance from the infamous Magnolia Bakery: a double-layered confection hand-decorated with frosting farm animals.

"I'm not a particularly domestic person." I laughed. "But ever since Anna's birth, sometimes I get this desire to do things like buy a sewing machine so I can design all her clothes. Or get a glue gun and redecorate the house. What is it about motherhood that inspires these crazy impulses?"

"Well, in my case, I realize now that I was compensating,"

Bronwyn said seriously. "I guess . . . for a long time, I thought I'd never have kids."

I nodded knowingly. "It seems like half the women I know had some trouble getting pregnant," I said.

"Oh, no," she said. "It wasn't that. It was just that I miscarried . . . before . . ."

"I'm sorry," I said.

She sat quietly for a moment, and I waited.

"Before Lloyd," she said finally. "With my first husband."

Slowly, as we sank deeply into the cushioned seats of the Rigatoni Factory Theater, she told me the story of her earlier life with Garrett. He had wanted to be a writer. Except that he couldn't write. Or at least he never managed to get anything on paper.

"Once, a long time ago, there was something special about him," Bronwyn said thoughtfully. "He was very smart and had some kind of talent. But when you leave it in there too long, I don't know, it turns ugly. He hated everything. He started hating me. . . ."

Bronwyn stopped for a moment, her lips suddenly strained tight, as though holding something in.

"The miscarriage happened after he pushed me down the stairs."

I gingerly put my hand on her arm and let it stay. Her bones were thin and light, like those of a bird.

"It's for the best," she said. "It wasn't meant to be. Then I met Lloyd, and we have two beautiful children. When Harrison was born, I just wanted to celebrate every minute of every day. For Harrison's first birthday party I . . . I actually rented out the Rainbow Room!"

She laughed gaily at herself, obviously relishing the memory of a blowout party for a one-year-old at the tippy-top of Rockefeller Center. I found myself rejoicing for her. She was one of those women who appeared to have had a perfect, blessed life. Now I knew the truth.

Suddenly, a frightened look passed across her eyes. "You know, I haven't told anyone at school I've been divorced," she said in a low voice. "It's not like it's a big secret, it's just that I'd rather . . ."

"I understand," I said, vowing privately that her story would be safe with me. Life at Metropolitan was complicated enough without worrying about how to explain an imperfect past.

While Bronwyn and I were chatting, I spotted Serena's mom walking up the aisle, accepting congratulations from the other parents.

"Eve Forsythe told me that she and Jeffrey were planning to stop by," I heard her say to a woman in a paisley shawl and pearl necklace.

"Oh, I'm sorry, I just spoke to Jeffrey," said Pearl Necklace. "He's stuck at a polo match. They won't be able to make it."

"Oh, that's too bad," Serena's mom replied with a forced smile.

Pearl Necklace fluttered off, her mission of social demotion evidently accomplished. The hostess dithered for a moment, then approached a young man in a catering uniform who had been fussing with the food and party decorations throughout the event.

"These balloons are not pink!" she hissed at him through gritted teeth. "I asked you to match them to the invitations, which are *pink*! *This*"—she batted a balloon with her hand—"is not pink."

"They are pink," the man said firmly. "Ish."

"They are *orange*!" She looked like she was going to blow.

"They are salmon," he shot back.

Before Serena's mom could decapitate her party decorator, the lights dimmed and the drumroll sounded again: Several caterers appeared with the lit birthday cake.

"The gift-giving at these things is definitely getting out of hand," Bronwyn murmured to me, allowing me a peek at the exquisite sequined children's gown she'd bought for Serena. "But what can I do? When I see these adorable things, I have to buy them for someone! Besides, if you don't play the game, nobody will come to your party!" Her eyes twinkled merrily. "So what did you get for Serena?" she whispered.

"Er, I got her a book. . . ." I started to explain. I caught a split-second look of alarm on Bronwyn's face. But further conversation was made impossible as everybody joined in a motley chorus of "Happy Birthday."

The birthday mother began officiating over the birthday cake, cutting a razor-thin sliver for her daughter before doling out thick slabs to all the other children. Then Serena and her mom began systematically working their way through each gift on the table, loudly cooing over adorable cashmere coats, elaborately dressed dolls, and silk pajama sets. After several minutes, they reached my store-wrapped book. I cringed.

"It's just a book," I heard Serena say, without opening it.

"Open it, dear!" her mom commanded with an icy smile.

While the girl ripped off the paper, the mom announced, "Oh, there's no card!" She snatched the book from her daughter and held it up high. "Whoever you are, thank you so much for the book!" she said with a snide smile. "Anybody care to claim it?"

Suddenly, Bronwyn stood up and loudly declared, "That's my gift!" She paused and glanced at the title of the book. "*Make Way for Ducklings*," she said simply. "It was my favorite book as a child."

Serena's mother's expression suddenly changed from sarcasm to saccharine respect. "Oh, thank you so much, Bronwyn. From one generation to the next." She flashed Bronwyn a grateful smile. "Such a thoughtful, heartfelt present. We will cherish it, truly."

As the pair turned to the other gifts on the table, Bronwyn sat back down and discreetly handed me her box from Barneys.

"Bronwyn, you didn't have to do that," I said in a low voice.

"Oh, I know," Bronwyn replied lightly. But we both knew something important had happened.

"You know, I really did love that book as a child," she added. We exchanged conspiratorial smiles. "Now go put your present in the pile, then come back here and keep me company," she said.

With the gift-opening ceremony now over, the kids and moms returned to a final burst of sugar-induced pandemonium in preparation for leaving. Serena's mom worked her way back toward Bronwyn and me. Along the way, she passed by Jake, who was busy turning his slice of cake into a form of mushy soup.

"Hi Jake," she said, patting his head. "You going to bring your mother next time?"

He grunted.

She plopped down in the seat next to me and leaned over to look past me at Bronwyn. "It was wonderful of you to come,

Bronwyn. And thank you so much for passing along your own favorite book. It's gifts like yours that mean the most."

"And thank *you* for the lovely dress," she said, turning to me. "So"—she took a deep breath—"I hear you're hard at work on the auction committee."

I nodded. *Who would she have heard that from?* I wondered. *Kim?*

"Well," she said, getting up and giving me that icy smile again. "Just let me know if there is anything I can do. I'm sure it can't be easy. I do hope Anna is feeling . . . *better*."

"Anna is fine!" I blurted out, but she was already walking away. Bronwyn looked at me with alarm.

"What was that about?" I asked her urgently.

"Kim," Bronwyn said, shaking her head slowly.

"What do you mean?"

"Kim knows Jake is the prime suspect. So she's looking for somebody else to take the fall."

"You don't mean that Kim is trying to spread rumors about *my* child?"

"She'll try to pin it on somebody, Laura," Bronwyn replied, looking squarely at me, sympathetic but firm. "My guess is that she'll go for the easy target first."

Chapter 3

Sugar and spice and everything nice,
That's what little girls are made of

I crossed the green triangle at the intersection of Duane and Reade streets and entered through the glass doors of Bloom, the famed members-only club for TriBeCa mothers. *New York* magazine had recently listed Bloom as "*the* place for alpha moms—where society mothers go to meet the people who will get their children into the school of their choice." The receptionist, a sleek, young brunette, greeted me with a frosty British accent. I could tell from her attitude that the club had had problems with gate-crashers in the past. When she learned I had a guest spot reserved for 9:15 a.m. Yoga Fusion, however, she nodded appreciatively and instructed me to sit in the waiting area by the front window. Yoga Fusion was the exercise class that had restored some of the most glamorous postpartum figures in the city.

I sat on a cream-colored sofa and looked at myself in a half-dozen reflections from various strategically placed mirrors. Exotic ferns sprouted from every corner, and my feet rested on a chocolate-brown carpet made of woven leather. Past the reception desk I could see Bloom's retail store, which offered exclusive lines of children's clothing, educational toys, baby gear, and high-end beauty products. Everything from the doorknobs to the shop displays seemed obsessively chic. The stylishness of the place seemed to press in on me, like so many people shouting, demanding to be recognized. For a moment, I had the impulse to get up and walk out. I wanted to go pick up Anna from school and head for the hills, maybe plunge into a local swimming hole, the kind of place where I'd never have to worry about the "it" bag of the season. But then where would I send her to school? That was the rub.

It was Bronwyn's idea that we all meet here, and it was she who had signed us up for the famous Yoga Fusion. Dominique, of course, was already a member of Bloom. She didn't usually come to exercise, she told me, but she had standing weekly appointments for facials, wraps, and pedicures.

I knew Bronwyn wanted to discuss Snowflake's murder with Dominique. She hadn't said so directly on the phone, but I could tell from her tone of voice. "I think we need to get a read on her" was how Bronwyn put it. I tried to put the matter in perspective. Maybe it was all just a mistake. Maybe Jake wasn't quite the problem Bronwyn thought he was. Hamsters are so small—it could have been an accident. But still, with the picture of Snowflake's inert body competing with Serena's mother's icy smile in the nightmare gallery of my mind, I couldn't quite relax.

I glanced out the window and spotted Dominique picking her way across the cobblestoned street, dramatically swathed in a cream-and-mauve cashmere knit poncho and over-the-knee suede boots. Just before entering, she paused, fished a piece of gum out of her mouth, and threw it vaguely in the direction of a pile of trash bags. It missed its intended target and hit a homeless man on the head. He stirred in protest, but Dominique was already through the door. The cool receptionist greeted her by name.

"She is with me," Dominique replied, fluttering her hand in my direction as the receptionist nodded. "Put her on my permanent guest list." The idea of a members-only club for mothers had always seemed sort of offensive. But now that I was included, I felt a secret guilty thrill.

In the skin tone–flattering light of the elevator, Dominique eyed my navy sweats. "You American women. Always exercising!" She lifted mock weights over her head. "I admire you for that," she added unconvincingly. "We French women never forget our femininity. It is probably why I never have any luck with American men.

"It is true!" she continued loudly, contradicting my expression of disbelief. "In France and Italy, the way men look at me makes me feel like a woman. American men ignore me. Perhaps I am living on the wrong continent."

The elevator opened onto the penthouse tearoom. Giant bamboo plants rose from a circular garden in the center of the room and extended up into the oversized skylight. Outside, I could see the sundeck, and beyond that the tar- and aluminum-colored roofs of TriBeCa. At the dozen or so widely spaced tables on the blond-wood floor, groups of polished-looking women chatted as they sipped skinny lattes and nibbled egg-white omelets, their eyes restlessly skimming the room. Trendy handbags dangled insouciantly from the backs of their chairs.

We took a seat at a small table by a window, and Dominique ordered an espresso. She stuck her lower lip out and blew stray locks off her forehead.

"Well, that was an interesting auction committee meeting the other day, wasn't it?" I ventured.

She shrugged her shoulders and said nothing. I caught snatches of the conversations swirling around us.

"I *love* those chunky layers on you," I heard a woman sitting behind me say. "You can't fool me, girlfriend, that's a five-hundred-dollar haircut!"

"The Dalens are so rich, you can't compete," a woman in a lacy blouse at the table next to us was telling her companion.

"Can't compete," the other woman echoed, nodding in agreement.

Again, Dominique blew her own dirty blond bangs off her face with an expression of ennui. She looked even more listless than usual.

"That's a great poncho. . . . Where did you get it?" I offered.

"I don't know," she said indifferently. "Isaac picks whatever he thinks looks good on me. I hate to shop. How can I go to all of those stores? It would be a full-time job."

The waiter returned with our drinks and ceremoniously placed them on the table. Dominique immediately tested the espresso.

"It tastes like . . . *black water* . . ." she announced, waving away the profusely apologetic waiter.

I sipped my tea in awkward silence.

"So, how is your acting going?" I asked in a final effort to restart the conversation.

It was as if I had hit upon the secret spring. Dominique's list-lessness became subtly yet distinctly more heightened, and she shot me a well-rehearsed look of despair.

"My acting career . . . it's over," she announced. "I should never have married. I should never have enchained myself to convention. I look at someone like Angelina Jolie. Now there is a woman with a *life*. She gets interesting roles, she can have any man she wants. She has children on her own terms! Now she travels all over the world, she has allure, she does what she wants. She is *living, loving*. I would like a life like that. I think, *Why her? Why not me?*"

Apart from the convenient editing that Dominique was using to eliminate the inevitable complications from the exploits of Angelina Jolie, there were several problems with this script. The few details I knew of Dominique's career suggested a far more glamorous existence than she liked to admit. A highly publicized catfight at the Hotel du Cap, allegations about a wild night in the Lincoln Bedroom, and her lawsuit against *Star* magazine over certain compromising photographs taken on a yacht in Saint-Tropez—all were the stuff of Metropolitan gossip. One year, she had been nominated for an Oscar as Best Supporting Actress. Another mother at Metropolitan had wryly observed that when she attended the same school tour as Dominique, none of the administrators had paid attention to any of the other candidates. But it evidently wasn't enough to satisfy Dominique.

"The only parts my agent calls me about now are voice-overs for luxury tissue paper," she continued, turning to me. "I told him I do not do toilets! I am an actress! I want something that reflects the real me."

"Like what?" I asked.

"I want to be Miss Julie again," she replied, looking at me meaningfully.

Now I understood why my high-school teacher, Mr. Odom—Odious Odom, we called him—had been put upon this Earth. Almost twenty years on, I could still remember being forced to regurgitate lines from August Strindberg's revolting piece of misogynistic theater.

"We will run away to Italy and open a hotel, my darling," I crooned, approximating the part of Miss Julie's love object, the lustful servant Jean.

Dominique's eyes widened briefly in surprise. Then she clicked into her role.

"But where will we get the money? When he discovers our love, my father will disown me!" she said, clutching my arm.

We locked eyes. Her face suddenly opened up to me.

"Laura," she whispered, genuine tears forming on her cheeks. "You understand me. How do you know Miss Julie so well?"

"Well, I'm a writer. . . ." I said.

"I knew it. I knew you were more than the island party girl! I can see the sadness in your eyes. We are alike, you and I. Artists!"

"I mean, I'm not a writer-writer, I'm a copywriter. . . ." I started to explain.

My point seemed to get lost in translation. "Communication!" she exclaimed. "It is so vital! And yet so difficult!"

As a freelance advertising copywriter, in fact, my job was all about helping clients communicate a very simple three-word message: Buy My Product!

"Well, it's not really——" I started.

"I wish I could write," she interrupted me. "Then I would tell the story of my life."

She started to unpack some well-rehearsed anecdotes about her rise to the top—or, as she saw it, the middle. She had enrolled in acting classes as a teenager and quickly drew the attention of a famous French director who cast her as a brooding ingénue. After that, she landed roles in a variety of French cinematic hits. But Dominique was determined to be a crossover success on the world stage. She moved to Hollywood with her first minor role in an American film, then to New York for a lead part on Broadway. "I was getting fantastic roles, having passionate affairs," she said with a sigh. "I was *recognized*!"

But her success in America never approached that of her career in Europe. Her French accent was indelible, which severely curtailed the roles she was offered. Shortly after losing the Oscar to Kate Hudson and getting pilloried in the press for her gypsy-look gown ("the spirit of Cher rides again!" the tabloids said), she met Alan.

"When I met him, we were both on fire," Dominique said with a laugh. "No, really, we were! The club was burning down!"

Her eyes sparkled. She had obviously told the story many times before, but she equally obviously relished telling it again. They were at a very exclusive nightclub in the meatpacking district. A flambé got out of hand, smoke filled the air, and everybody rushed for the exit. She felt a hand on her shoulder, and a man guided her through a long back passage lit only by flashing red lights. When they reached the street, he held her and they kissed.

Then came marriage and baby.

"Now, I am just a woman," she said. "Not even. I am a *wife*! That must be the ugliest word in your language! And I have been a good wife to Alan." She sighed, as though it were an admission of personal failure.

Alan was a successful developer of upscale suburban shopping malls. "These places where people go to do their exercise in the morning, walking around and around . . ." Dominique shuddered. "Alan is a good man. When he says he is staying late at the office, it is because he is staying late at the office. I respect that, you know. But there is no passion in my life!"

Now fully enmeshed in her own private melodrama, she brushed aside my words of consolation. I thought about how Richard and I had met in graduate school. After my long and turbulent flight through urban singledom, Richard had been like a safe landing at a quiet country airport. Little had I known what drama awaited. Having a child was like giving birth to a little hurricane, able to blow full-sized grown-ups right off their feet.

I could see that Dominique, on the other hand, loved being caught in a storm. She had mistaken Alan for a romantic lead in a costume epic. She wanted to be rescued from burning buildings,

defended from menacing crowds, proudly escorted to a midnight
ball at the palace. Instead, he'd bought her a country house in
Greenwich, Connecticut.

"I am a good mother," Dominique continued. "But I take no
satisfaction in it."

She paused and cast her eyes down, her body shaking almost
imperceptibly, like Miss Julie in her final scene, just before she
commits suicide.

"Laura, I am *suffocating*! I am a woman who *lives for love*!" She
looked up at me and blinked. "In France, you know, these things
are much better understood."

It struck me that Dominique was the kind of European who is
more American than she makes herself out to be. Unlike any
other French person I'd met, she had no trouble confiding her in-
nermost thoughts to strangers, for example, or having the loud-
est voice in the room.

Dominique looked at me fiercely, as though demanding that I
find for her the passion that was missing in her life. But suddenly,
the door of the tearoom burst open and Bronwyn appeared over
our table. Her tight, blond ponytail fell straight down the middle
of the back of her workout jacket.

"So there you are!" she said with an expression of disbelief.
"I've been looking all over for you guys! Yoga Fusion has already
started! C'mon!"

She raced out of the room and we followed her down the
stairs. We dashed past a charming playroom where a pair of young
Latina women watched over a half-dozen two-year-olds and
rushed into the yoga studio. The class was already under way. The

mirrors on opposite walls created an eerie tunnel effect, and the hard beechwood floor broadcast each of our footsteps like gunshots.

The instructor, a sinewy man in his early thirties, had chiseled features and, improbably, a short, high ponytail of the type you'd see on a little girl. He somberly inclined his head to acknowledge our arrival.

Bronwyn, Dominique, and I slipped silently into the Downward Dog position along with the rest of the class. As my head dangled upside down, I glanced around slyly at the other women around me. Their skin was pink and smooth; their teeth were white and square; their figures were enviable. They had the kind of sleek good looks that suggest only the most subtle of surgical modifications.

Bronwyn moved into all the poses with expert precision. She was fit and athletic—thanks to thrice-weekly sessions with a personal trainer. Dominique possessed a Frenchwoman's neat physique that spoke of portion control and a smoking habit, but she was clearly unaccustomed to challenging her body into deep stretches. She seemed to take the instructor's words as merely helpful suggestions. From time to time, he would come over and adjust her posture. She responded by shooting him a calculated look of innocent gratitude from behind her mascara.

The class ended and the other women filed out quickly. But Dominique lingered. She approached the instructor and put her finger lightly on a tattoo on his left arm. It was an odd geometric pattern made up of orange triangles inside a blue square. "What is it?" she asked, her finger tracing the slightly faded lines.

"Ah, how ironical," he said. "Most people notice the other one." He gestured to his right arm, which had a tattoo of a phoenix. "This one is very symbolical for me. But it can't be put it into words." He closed his eyes as though bearing a silent pain.

"Oh," Dominique said coquettishly. "There are so many things that cannot be put into words!"

The yoga instructor was about to say something, but just then Bronwyn approached and took Dominique firmly by the arm. It was time to leave. Dominique turned to wave good-bye.

"Why are you making me rush out like that?" Dominique said, turning to Bronwyn with a giggle. "He is a very attractive man. I wonder if he gives private classes!"

"He's currently giving them to *several* Metropolitan moms," Bronwyn snapped.

Dominique raised her eyebrows but said nothing.

The changing room was accented with warm teak and smelled like geraniums. Potted orchids graced travertine countertops, and the shower stalls featured tile mosaics and brushed-nickel fixtures. The shelves were stocked with jars of exotically scented potions from Bliss Spa. Attendants moved silently through the spa, whisking white towels off the floor and brandishing bottles of mineral water. Women padded in and out of the steam room and sauna. Others lounged in the whirlpool. Dominique and I sat down on a plush terry-cloth banquette while Bronwyn opened her locker.

From the banquette, Bronwyn looked tall and confident, every inch the top mom of the school. She cloaked herself in a bathrobe and gave us a smile as she headed off for the shower.

Dominique and I exchanged glances.

"So, what did you make of . . . Snowflake's demise?" I asked her quietly. The horrible vision of Snowflake's twisted neck zoomed back up in my mind. I pictured a child—*Jake?*—grabbing the poor hamster while nobody was looking, then snapping, crushing, twisting.

"Snowflake?"

"The hamster."

"You know it was one of the boys," Dominique said nonchalantly. "Only a boy would kill an innocent animal. Girls are not so aggressive."

I nodded, though I wasn't so sure about her logic. I'd seen some pretty vicious girls on the playgrounds—hogging the swings, grabbing other kids' toys, and all the rest.

"Hey, maybe it was just an accident," I said to Dominique.

Dominique shook her head. "No," she said firmly. "It is no accident. That is what boys—what men—do. They fight. They kill. They like death. Maybe even more than sex."

Bronwyn returned from her shower with a towel wrapped around her head. She could not have overheard our conversation, yet she seemed to know exactly what we had been talking about.

"I'm so lucky to have a boy like Harrison," she said, rubbing her flaxen hair vigorously with the towel. "He is so gentle."

She paused.

"He loves taking care of his baby sister."

We sat in silence for a moment.

"So, what did you think of Kim's boy's little behavioral problem?" she said to Dominique, affixing large pearl studs onto each earlobe. One of them slipped from her hand and landed with a clatter on the travertine countertop.

The question hovered in the air. Dominique and I looked at each other uncertainly.

"You know it was him?" Dominique asked doubtfully.

"Oh my God, everybody knows," Bronwyn said, grimacing as she latched the errant pearl in place. "Jake has some serious issues."

"Oh," Dominique said, seeming to lose interest.

"It gets worse," Bronwyn continued. "I think Kim is trying to pin the blame on one of our kids. She'll do anything to get into Holyfield!"

Dominique started to perk up. "What? She cannot possibly blame Emmy. That is outrageous!"

"I don't think it's Emmy she'll go for," Bronwyn said, looking at me. "I don't know, but I think maybe she's trying to spread rumors about Anna."

Dominique shot up from the banquette, her hands pressed to her cheeks. "The injustice!" she practically shouted. It was Miss Julie, ardently rebelling against the confines of patriarchy and social class.

"Do you really think that's what she's doing?" I asked Bronwyn.

"I just have a good hunch," Bronwyn added.

"No! Do not deceive yourselves," Dominique pleaded. "I know this kind of woman! I have seen her type before. She would kill a dozen rats to get her way! She is dangerous!"

Any doubts Bronwyn and I had reserved about Kim vanished in the wake of Dominique's passionate certainty.

"She will do anything to get her kid into Holyfield," Bronwyn exclaimed.

"I can't believe she'd actually do that!" I added. "Trying to blame Anna!"

"She must be stopped!" Dominique said. "Oh, Laura." She turned to me with tears in her eyes. "Do not give up! We must protect you!"

"We've got to work together on this," Bronwyn declared.

I left the Bloom Club feeling daunted by the grave challenge that lay ahead and yet reassured and invigorated, happy in the knowledge that Bronwyn, Dominique, and I were now a team.

Chapter 4

Up above the world so high
Like a diamond in the sky

The evening sky over Wall Street was a canopy of pink and blue. I looked out on the jumbled downtown skyline, feeling like I owned New York. Off in the distance, Staten Island and the New Jersey waterfront formed a single long, thin silhouette, a dim but persistent reminder that there was life outside the city. Just to my left, the large, illuminated clock on the Tribeca Grand hotel marked the hour in roman numerals. I sipped champagne and let the crisp fall breeze blow through my hair. I was glad I had decided to change out of the yellow sleeveless cocktail dress and into my never-fail black trousers and V-neck sweater.

The autumn twilight air somehow helped dispel the doubts that had sprung up in my mind after Bronwyn's parting words at Bloom. The night before, I had lain awake in bed, wondering if Kim would really try to fob off the blame for Snowflake's death on Anna. But now, as I sipped my champagne, it all seemed so far-fetched. Richard was right: It was just a school, they were just ordinary people, and the flattering neckline of my trusty black cashmere sweater still offered a hint of subtle sex appeal. I took in a deep breath and turned to face Metropolitan's parents-only get-acquainted party on the rooftop terrace of Emilio and Pilar's loft on Franklin Street.

"On the family's estate in Cuba—you know, my grandfather was a count—they kept an enormous stable," Emilio had said, waving at a table of trophies and other equestrian paraphernalia as he was guiding us through the loft's foyer downstairs. "So as soon as I got to Phillips Exeter Academy, I joined the polo team. . . ."

To judge by real estate, Emilio and Pilar were among the wealthier parents at Metropolitan. They were discreetly listed on a school brochure as "Friends of Metropolitan," which meant that they gave more to the school in donations than they did in tuition. It was Emilio who was responsible for introducing Jeffrey and Eve Forsythe, the school's grandest benefactors, to the Metropolitan community, all the more notable in their generosity because they were childless. Emilio and Jeffrey played polo together, as Emilio was careful to let every guest know.

"*Amor,*" Pilar said, pulling Emilio away. She was a lanky Venezuelan oil heiress with reddish-brown hair, improbably pert breasts, and a permanent pout on her lips, which looked vaguely unnatural. Tonight she was tottering around in a taupe silk dress, which was cut so deep in the back that you could see butt cleavage.

"There is someone for you to meet." She gave Richard and me a quick, silent look-over as she yanked her husband away.

I heard Emilio begin the same story with the next round of guests. "On the family's estate in Cuba—you know, my grandfather was a count . . ."

Up on the roof terrace, the red-and-gold panels of a Moorish-style tent wafted in the breeze, revealing a world of embroidered cushions, plush stools, and ornate brass tea-sets inside. The scene was illuminated with flickering candlelight in elaborate Moroccan sconces. On one edge of the tent stretched a long table piled high with kebabs arranged in architectural patterns. Just outside the tent, a clear-glass skylight offered a view of the loft below, whose brocaded curtains, antique furniture, and vaulted walls decorated with a collection of minor old master paintings made it seem like the imperial capital to the giddy colonial outpost on the roof.

Metropolitan parents circled one another, exchanging condensed life stories and silently assessing the value of Emilio and Pilar's stupendous parcel of real estate while waiters in flowing white kaftans poured drinks and proffered trays of pistachio-crusted salmon tips and spiced lamb in puff pastry. Everything was in its place.

Except, possibly, my husband. Before the party, I had pestered him to put on "something nice." Grudgingly, he had donned his "formal" outfit, the old brown suit he wore to official university functions. He couldn't find his formal shoes, so he put on hiking boots. The ones with the red laces.

"What?" he said, when I gave his boots a despairing look.

I reached for my husband and drew him close to me.

"Now, you *know* you're going to be the sexiest guy at the party," I chided my husband teasingly, "so you already have a *huge* advantage over all those boring Wall Street stiffs. But if, in addition to your superior physical charms, you show up in your Montana Mountain He-Man hiking boots, you're gonna drive all those Wall Street widows mad with lust—"

"Okay, okay," he cut me off jokingly. "If you want me to find my other shoes, just give me a couple minutes in the closet."

"I'll help you." I joined him. Wondering what to wear myself, I held out a hanger with the fanciest dress I owned—a sleeveless vintage cocktail number in a bright buttercup yellow. In fact, it had been my mother's dress, a souvenir from her years as a 1950s party girl. She'd bought it at Jacqueline's of Beverly Hills and had a pair of shoes dyed to match. I'd discovered the frock languishing in her attic a few years ago and updated it by shortening the hem an inch or two. It was still in great condition. I looked at it skeptically.

"Hey, Richard?" I asked him. "Should I wear this dress? Or would basic black be more appropriate?"

He eyed me with a mischievous smile. "I don't know. Turn around." I rotated flirtatiously.

"You know," he mused, "you look hot in everything you wear. So hot I just can't wait to take it off you . . ."

I reached for Richard and gave him a squeeze. My husband might be the only Metropolitan papa with only a single suit in his closet, but at least he didn't give a damn what I wore.

I stripped off my jeans, and Richard tried to pull me over to the bed.

"Not now, baby!" I giggled but remained firm, reaching for my black trousers and sweater and pulling them on. "This is an important party and I don't want to be late."

"Suit yourself." He shrugged.

From the moment we arrived on the roof terrace, Richard had parked himself in front of the kebab table. He remained there, motionless, as though trying to ward off fellow guests from his private hoard of goodies. I plucked a glass of champagne off a silver tray and decided to leave him to his own devices.

I sensed a commotion. It was Dominique, stepping out of the staircase bulkhead as though she was coming out onstage. She was dressed to match her surroundings in a gauzy floor-length skirt and midriff-baring sequined top. In one hand she carried a glass of wine, which she raised to her lips every few seconds with practiced flair. With her other hand she held the arm of her husband, Alan. He was tall and good-looking in a square-jawed way, and wore a well-cut suit with a striped tie. She spotted me and whirled over.

"Now, this is the way to *live*," Dominique said, opening her arms up to the circus-sized tent.

She introduced me to Alan and we shook hands.

"Great to meet you, Laura," he said with a faint Midwestern accent.

"Where is your husband?" Dominique demanded.

I gestured toward Richard by the hors d'oeuvres.

"Alan, he looks lost. Go and talk to him!" Dominique ordered her husband. With a mock salute, he headed off in Richard's direction.

Dominique glanced around with bright eyes, like a restless schoolgirl looking for mischief. I couldn't help but remember her comments at Bloom about her dissatisfaction with her life. I glanced at Alan, who was now shaking hands with Richard. He seemed nice enough, but what did I know? Some acquaintance caught Dominique's attention, and she flitted away, saying, "We must have fun tonight, Laura!"

I found myself next to a cluster of a half-dozen women gathered around the pouting, statuesque Pilar. I recognized Serena's mommy, and a few other women whose kids were in Anna's class. Like most of the Metropolitan moms, they were a physically impressive lot—fit and well-mannered, with shiny hair and shiny fingernails. They wore conversation-worthy necklaces, neat silk dresses, and embellished cardigans paired with well-cut skirts and trousers. It was obvious in an instant that these were the stay-at-home mothers of Metropolitan, the ones who dominated the school's field trips and its social scene. The most distressing thing about them was that none of them looked tired. Taking care of my wolf-child, juggling household tasks, and clinging to my freelance career had left permanent, droopy half-moons under my eyes.

"All Orson will eat these days is potatoes and pasta," a woman in a full skirt and gold slipper flats was confiding to the others.

"I've taken my daughter off carbs completely," replied Serena's mother, now wearing a silk-wrap print dress.

"It is the only way." Pilar nodded in agreement, rubbing her prominent clavicles. "At Chanterelle, even the children's menu has grilled fish and steamed vegetables. They understand people who want to eat healthy. . . ."

"I've heard of this new book. It's called *Taming Toddler Tantrums at the Table,*" I said, attempting to step into the conversation. "They say it's pretty good."

The ladies smiled politely and coolly watched my comment hang in the air for a few moments before allowing it to dissipate into the evening sky.

Just when the pause had reached the point where I was considering whether to fall into a faint, shout "Free Angela Davis!" or simply slink away, I felt a hand pulling on my shoulder. I turned to see Bronwyn in a pale blue dress and matching headband. Her ice-blond hair was styled to perfection. The other women greeted her with the kind of warmth that midtown Manhattan maître d's bring out for billionaires.

"Everybody, this is *Laura,*" Bronwyn said.

"Yes, I remember," said Serena's mother, offering a slightly defrosted version of her icy smile.

"Of course," said Slipper Flats, looking at me with sudden interest. "From the auction committee. We were just talking about our kids' insane eating habits."

"How is Lloyd?" Pilar asked Bronwyn. "I saw his picture in the business section the other day."

"He's just racking up those frequent-flier miles," Bronwyn replied with a note of feigned despair.

"Anyway, I know what you mean about toddler appetites," she continued self-deprecatingly. "Harrison eats so much better when he's with Bernadette. Those West Indian women have a way with kids."

"Well, I used to think so, too," said Pilar. "But once you go Tibetan, you *never* go back."

"I should get a Tibetan," said Pearl Necklace. "The minute I'm out the door, Deborah plugs the kids into the TV. And can anyone tell me why nannies are so surly? Deborah makes four hundred fifty dollars a week, *cash in hand*. Then she demands extra pay to come with us to the Hamptons. *The Hamptons!*"

"A lot of my friends uptown are hiring Chinese nannies," Serena's mother said. "Because, you know, China's on the rise. They think it'll give the kids an edge in business."

"I've heard that from some of my uptown friends, too," Pearl Necklace said. "The problem is, most of the Chinese nannies in New York speak *Cantonese*." She and Serena's mother exchanged meaningful looks.

"That is a problem," Pilar said.

"I know it sounds crazy," Slipper Flats announced somberly, "but I'm thinking of getting rid of our nanny altogether."

"Oooooohhhhh!" The others made noises of alarm.

"How long have you had your nanny, Laura?" Slipper Flats turned to me solicitously, clearly hoping to cover her back in case I turned out to be more of a contender than my appearance suggested.

Bronwyn shot me a reassuring look.

"Well . . . I've never had one," I said. "But . . . we have a babysitter from time to time. Like tonight." There was another brief pause as the other women silently digested this information, making an effort not to reveal their scorn this time.

"I think that's great," Pearl Necklace said. "The other day, I took Anabelle to the park myself. I was the only mommy there. I felt . . . earthy. Like I was baking bread from scratch."

I sipped my champagne nonchalantly and tried to sharpen up a verbal stiletto. But my wits were a little dulled by the drink. I decided to check out of the conversation. Pretending to feel a buzz in my pocket, I flipped open my cell phone and mumbled something about the sitter as I retreated from the group.

This had an almost immediate impact, although not the one I was aiming for, since I backed directly into a waiter, who was fortunately between drink- and food-laden tray circuits. He was wearing a white caftan, with a brickred fez perched atop his frizzy blond hair. He looked to be about thirty. *Probably an out-of-work actor,* I thought to myself. He had his hand on the pole that held up the tent at its center and was eyeing it uneasily. We apologized simultaneously, then went our separate ways. Drifting to the other side of the tent, I caught snatches of the conversations swirling around me.

"This Christmas we're checking out Crested Butte for a change," said a woman with a flowered handbag. "It's not Aspen, but the kids' program is *incredible*. . . ."

"So we're leveraging foreign currencies against the falling dollar . . ." a stocky man was explaining to a small group of men in business suits.

"We booked a suite at the Four Seasons," boasted a woman with stringy hair and a Texas twang. "It cost us thirty grand for two weeks, but it was totally baby-proofed. 'Cause, you know, Gwyneth Paltrow had stayed there a few months earlier with Apple. . . ."

I plucked a date stuffed with ground beef off one of the silver trays and popped it into my mouth, titillated by the heady combination of sweet and spicy flavors. I found myself bumping up against another small clutch of women. They were more soberly dressed than the first group, and their faces were less elaborately made up.

"God, she amazes me," an energetic-looking blonde with short hair was saying. "Next thing you know, they'll have her running a bake sale. I'm like, hey, how about if I just *give* the school my money?"

"Tell me about it," replied a tall, freckled woman in a taupe jacket. "Who has the time?"

The high-octane blonde jerked her head in the direction of the stay-at-home women's club, and the tall, freckled woman smirked in acknowledgment.

"I mean, if I told my boss I was cutting out early for a school fund-raising meeting, he'd put me on the endangered species list," the blonde woman continued.

"Yeah, but what if it was for a golf game?" The women exchanged a bitter laugh.

I felt a surge of working-women's solidarity. I knew all about the golf factor. I once sat down with my slightly older officemate, Gail, and worked out how much golf could have added to her income in the form of undeserved promotions and profitable schmoozes if she hadn't spent the time raising her two teenagers.

I was about to attempt to join the conversation when the women stepped apart to make room for Kim, wearing a dark pinstripe jacket and skirt. She was just putting her BlackBerry back in its sheath. As she looked up and saw me, a barely perceptible flash of suspicion crossed her face. The other women seemed to register my presence for the first time.

From across the room, I caught Bronwyn shooting me a warning look. I decided to take another phone call. As I moved away, pretending to be lost in another absorbing conversation with my voicemail, I heard the tall, freckled woman whisper to Kim, "Who was that?"

"You mean the woman in black? That's *Laura*."

I cringed. Earlier, I had felt chic and cool in my never-fail outfit. Now, as I looked around the terrace, I realized that nobody else was wearing all black. Even the working mothers had figured out how to deck themselves in alluring combinations of color and texture. Their outfits said: "I'm grown up, sophisticated, and upbeat. I listen to Starbucks-approved selections of world music on the iPod my husband gave me for my last birthday, along with that citrine cocktail ring from Bulgari." *My* outfit said: "I mope around the house listening to Velvet Underground and Joy Division. I'm living in the past and *I'm a total loser*."

I again wandered off, my despair mounting. I caught sight of Dominique at the other end of the room; it appeared as though she was flirting with a pair of Metropolitan papas. Suddenly I tripped, hard, into the pole in the center of the tent. To my horror, the pole shifted out of its socket, and I felt a slight tremor pass through it. I gripped the pole mightily and tried to pull it back to center. Had I somehow broken the pole? I caught the eyes of the same frizzy-haired waiter I'd bumped into before, and he gave me an odd expression. I looked around desperately for my husband.

He was still standing by the hors d'oeuvres table, but, to my surprise, he was chatting merrily with a petite woman wearing a sleeveless yellow cocktail dress, pretty much like the one I now wished I had put on before the party.

Richard turned to look at me a little awkwardly. He was up to something. I could always tell.

I signaled with fiery eyes for him to come to my aid. He shuffled over with his new friend in tow.

"Laura, this is Amy," he said as they reached me. My knuckles were white on the pole. Amy was a fair-haired woman with hazel eyes, a small nose, and oversized diamond studs on her earlobes. She was fastidiously groomed, almost comically conservative. Neither of them seemed to notice that I was holding up the tent with one arm. Amy reached out to shake my hand.

I glanced down at the base of the pole and decided that it was close enough to the socket to stay in place. I released my grip gently. To my relief, the tent did not collapse. I took Amy's hand in my palm, which was now coated with a bizarre mix of sweat and wood polish.

"Nice to meet you, Amy," I said. She smiled back.

"I was just telling Richard that he looks exactly the same after all these years," she said gaily. She turned to Richard and gave a bright little laugh. "You haven't aged a bit. I'm sure there's a portrait of Dorian Gray hanging somewhere in your house!"

I turned to my husband with a questioning look.

"Yeah." He shuffled uncomfortably. "You know . . . We went to college together. . . ."

It hit me: This was *Amy,* Richard's college girlfriend.

"Amy?" I said, unable to hide my incredulity. From the occasional story Richard had passed on about his one great flame (before I lit up his heavens, he assured me), I had always pictured Amy as a long-haired bohemian type. They met sophomore year, studied classics together, and spent a summer biking along the coast of Australia. How bad could she be? Then they got accepted to graduate schools in different cities. He went east, she went midwest; their relationship fizzled. *She's supposed to be teaching* Beowulf *to farmers' kids in Oklahoma!* I thought, dismayed. *What is she doing here, looking like a rich New York housewife?*

"Richard has been telling me all about you," Amy said coyly. "Isn't it such an amazing coincidence to meet up after all these years—in *preschool?*" She spread her arms awkwardly, gesturing around the room.

I tried for a conciliatory smile. Richard hurriedly filled me in on what he had learned. Amy was married. She nodded in the direction of a man in his late forties with bad skin and a pinstripe suit chatting with some other parents by the bar. Wesley was a partner in a midwestern accounting firm and had recently taken on the assignment of opening an office in New York.

"Wesley's a CPA," Amy said.

"A sepia?" I said, confused. "Isn't that a kind of squid?"

"An accountant." Richard smirked. Amy giggled. It felt like two against one—the wrong two. I felt a surge of anger.

"Anyway," Amy said, "I hope our daughters will play together."

"Is your daughter also in Tori's class?" I asked with dread.

"Uh, yeah . . ." Richard gave me a frightened look.

"Oh, yes," Amy said brightly. "Anna loves Tori!"

"Anna?" I said. "I mean, I know Anna *likes* Tori, but I'm not sure she . . ."

"No," Amy said, with a nervous giggle. "I mean *my* Anna."

Richard looked at me with big rabbit eyes—a rabbit seeing the headlights of an oncoming car.

I stared at them in mute horror. The subject of our daughter's name had finally been declared off-limits territory for the safety and common good of the household, if not the community. It had taken almost until Anna's first birthday for me to finally reconcile myself to the name Richard had foisted upon my daughter. As a "Laura," I had wanted to bestow something a little more original on my precious child. Now the anger I had felt in those long months after our daughter's birth, every time I remembered how Richard had pressed his choice on me in the hospital—it all came back. What was worse, to find that this was his ex-girlfriend's choice . . .

Goaded by my inner masochist, I imagined a scene from long ago. On a cold January night, in a charming log cabin somewhere in New England, they had made love on a bearskin rug in front of a roaring fireplace. When their epic lust had been quenched, and with the fire reduced to glowing embers, Amy looked into Richard's eyes and said, "When we have a girl, we'll name her Anna."

"Anna," Richard had replied happily, then reached for her again. . . .

"Isn't it an amazing coincidence?" Amy exclaimed, snapping me into the present. "It was my husband's idea. He wouldn't listen to anything else."

She and Richard exchanged glances. I got the distinct feeling they were in cahoots.

I glowered at Richard.

"What?" he mouthed silently.

I felt a hand on my arm. Bronwyn was taking her guard duty seriously. She pointed to the staircase. "It's Jeffrey and Eve Forsythe," she said breathlessly.

The handsome couple appeared at the top of the stairs, tall and stylish, with an unmistakable air of affluence. My first thought was how attractive Jeffrey was. He had a slightly angular face and quick, dark eyes. I'd expected the benefactor of Metropolitan to look more paunchy and established, a bit like Amy's husband, Wesley. But Jeffrey wore a look of bemusement. He exuded hapless charm and Wall Street energy all at once, like Hugh Grant cast as a high-rolling chief executive.

From what Bronwyn had told me, I gathered that Jeffrey was of Australian origin but had made his fortune in South Africa. He was new to New York, but that was nothing bad in a town where the new were often wealthier than the old. Although he and Eve had no children, they were said to be "in the latter stages of adopting twins from Sri Lanka," a fact that was frequently offered in rebuttal to those bold enough to wonder about their especially keen interest in the Metropolitan preschool.

Eve was voluptuous and ethereal, with a pale complexion set off by dark brown hair and a rosebud mouth. She was probably my age, but somehow she both looked younger and felt older. She wore a gauzy, off-white sheath and a pale cashmere wrap shot through with silver. Even from across the tent, I could see the dazzling yellow sapphire necklace glowing against the rich cream of her dress.

As the school's special benefactors made their way toward the center of the tent, Metropolitan parents subtly maneuvered to position themselves within conversational range. Kim, looking severe and determined, reached Jeffrey first and caught him for a private conversation. I saw her pull out her BlackBerry and start typing, even as she and Jeffrey exchanged confidential whispers.

"Gansevoort, eleven a.m. Wednesday," I heard her say. "Excellent."

But this colloquy was quickly interrupted. Within seconds, the Forsythes were at the center of a large circle of people, with Emilio and Pilar attempting to act as emcees.

Bronwyn stepped forward, exulting like a bridge player holding all trumps. "This is Laura," she said to Eve, holding me by one arm. "She is the mother of *Anna*. The Forsythe Scholarship recipient."

"Wonderful!" Eve replied in a vaguely transatlantic accent. The two women beamed at each other with philanthropic bonhomie. "I do hope *Anna* is prospering at Metropolitan."

I felt a pair of eyes scrutinizing me, lifting the folds of my sweater and examining the contents. I locked gazes with Jeffrey. There was something haunting in his look, I thought, a hint of some yearning unfulfilled. Our eye contact lasted just an instant longer than would have been polite. My face felt warm. I looked away, wondering if anyone else had intercepted our exchange.

"All the kids love it there," Kim was saying to Eve, trying to jump back into the fray from her position next to the tent pole.

The energetic blonde and the tall, freckled woman were standing right behind her.

"Harrison especially!" Bronwyn added. "He can't stop talking about his teachers. I think he's got a crush on Tori!" Pearl Necklace and Slipper Flats were lined up at her back.

"I'm sure *they* can't stop talking about *him*, either," Kim said sweetly, turning to face her rival.

Bronwyn looked stunned for a moment but swiftly recovered. "That's a nice suit," she said, turning to Kim with a great white smile. "Did you come straight from the office?"

"Yes . . ."

"Wow. I remember those days, working all the time, all those late nights. But now that I have kids, I think it's really important to be there for them."

"I think it's important for children to have strong role models," Kim said without an instant's hesitation. "It certainly works for Jake. He's not the kind of kid who . . . *acts out*. . . ."

"Really," Bronwyn replied. "Then I guess he's benefiting from that *special* place you take him to."

Kim spat bullets with her eyes.

"It's so wonderful to see kids grow up and become independent beings," Eve interjected dreamily, apparently oblivious to the brewing conflict.

"So, are you having Harrison evaluated?" Kim asked Bronwyn with a well-calibrated note of concern in her voice.

Bronwyn's eyes popped open as though she had been slapped. "Evaluated? For what?"

"Oh, I'm sorry! It's just that I thought that after last week . . ."

"Have you had *your* boy evaluated?" Bronwyn interrupted, finally snapping.

A grim silence had descended over the rest of the rooftop. All faces were turned in our direction, as though watching a car crash in slow motion.

"Jake? Jake is not a—"

"A *murderer!*" Dominique blurted out at the front of the crowd, as though she was thinking aloud. She had joined the throng along with everyone else and apparently had been waiting for a propitious cue to make a dramatic entrance.

I glared at Kim, still stinging from her insinuating comment about my all-black outfit, the conversation about nannies, and the extremely vexing mental picture of Amy and Richard lying together on a bearskin rug in front of a fire.

"There's nothing wrong with getting professional help," I interjected a little hotly, taking Bronwyn's side.

Kim held me in her fierce gaze.

"The children most at risk are those from disadvantaged backgrounds," she hissed.

"What the . . . excuse me?" I said leaning forward, furious. Bronwyn's prediction had come true. Kim was turning on the weakest link—me.

Kim stepped back—right into the pole at the center of the tent. I looked down and saw it sliding away from its socket. A shudder passed through the tent's gilded roof. In a flash, I knew that the structure was about fall and that I would get the blame. *If only that waiter hadn't seen me!* I lunged toward the pole to stop it from slipping any further.

Kim saw me leaping toward her.

"Crazy bitch!" she screamed, raising her arms and deflecting me from my course.

I was in midair, entirely out of control, when I hit the pole. I hooked it with my elbow and felt it break free of its moorings as I took it down with me. A chorus of panicked screams and shouts of indignation filled the air as the dark tent roof descended gently over the entire party.

Chapter 5

Humpty Dumpty sat on a wall
Humpty Dumpty had a great fall

My laptop was perched unevenly on a stack of magazines, which rested on a "desk" that was in reality a night table with a bad leg, squeezed between the bed and a closet. This was my "office." Richard was playing with Anna in the part of our apartment that we had designated the "living area." Since the only thing that separated the living area from the office was a set of cardboard storage boxes—I sometimes had fantasies about The Container Store that were as intense as a secret crush—the living area was a space defined mainly in our minds.

That is, with the exception of Anna, in whose mind boundaries of every kind were there to be acknowledged or ignored at her convenience. Every few minutes she ran over to my side of the apartment, clambering over the boxes and all the rest of the clutter. Then she climbed into my lap and reached for the keyboard.

Ordinarily, I didn't attempt to write while Anna was around. But today she was staying home from school.

Following the tent-pole fiasco of last night, I had been too embarrassed to face the other mothers at drop-off. Besides, I told myself, there was no time to take Anna to school; I had a deadline I couldn't ignore.

"My cat-cow friend is very good at using the computer!" Anna announced. She had recently acquired an "imaginary friend" who she described as a "cat-cow who is very brave."

"That's wonderful," I said. "Just make sure she doesn't try to use this one. Now please, darling, Mommy has to work, or we'll all starve to death!"

"Waah," she said, in her imitation baby voice. "Waah. Cat-cow baby wants boppy!" *Boppy* was her word for breast milk. I'd weaned her at fourteen months, but somehow she still remembered breast-feeding and occasionally tried to feel me up.

I moved her hands away from the danger zone between my mammaries and the keyboard. My job was on the line.

"Could you please entertain your daughter?" I said to Richard, who was on the couch grading papers. "You said you'd take her this morning!"

"Alright, alright," he said impatiently. "It's not my fault if she always wants Mommy." He put a plate of scrambled eggs and bacon down on the middle of the floor, where I knew it would inevitably be mistaken for a small area rug by a stray foot. Richard's periodic promises to "pitch in with the housework" turned out to be as bankable as a vow from Winnie the Pooh to stay away from the honey jar. Before Anna's arrival, his innate slovenliness hadn't bothered me so much. But now my patience was wearing thin. Failing to keep Anna entertained *and* leaving scrambled eggs exposed to foot traffic *and* chatting with ex-girlfriends who steal the names of daughters—altogether, the picture was looking grim.

I willed myself to retreat into the tiny bit of mental space I reserved for work. I had a campaign theme to develop. I was studying Caribbean travel brochures intensively, trying desperately to come up with a marketing package for the Sun & Frolic Resort on the east side of Providenciales in the Turks and Caicos. My new boss, Carter, had passed it along as a plum assignment. "It's a little bit down-market from the Cheetah project," he explained, referring to the monster sports car whose advertising success I could claim some credit for. "Sun and Frolic is where people go when they hit the jackpot at the penny slots in Vegas. But it's huge. Imagine a stack of two thousand cardboard boxes, with a beach on one side and an airport on the other. But as our resident Caribbean expert, it'll be a cinch for you. I bet you can knock it off in a couple hours!"

It was my job to turn in a proposal for a marketing campaign—but I'd already missed the deadline. I was falling hopelessly behind.

"Come for the sun or just come for a frolic!"

"Because vacations are supposed to be fun!"

"It's how families are made!"

"Where the only screams you'll hear are from the seagulls!"

No! No! No! I was getting nowhere! I maniacally flipped through the stack of brochures, but the bland, smiling models in the promotional photos were as uninspiring as my useless slogan ideas. I closed my eyes, willing myself into the Caribbean, but the only scenes I could picture were of sunburned and corpulent masses pounding the margaritas to cope with cranky spouses and obnoxious kids.

While I was stewing in the cheap cocktails of my imagination, the telephone rang. It was the sand vendor. My other full-time job—volunteer set designer for the Metropolitan auction—had come to this. In an emergency telephone conference call meeting of the auction committee—minus Kim, who was out of town on business—Bronwyn had pushed a "resolution" to forge ahead with my suggestion of creating an artificial island, complete with sand, fake palm trees, tropical rum punches, and Caribbean dancers.

"Look, lady, I ain't got all day. I need to know what kinda sand you want," the voice on the phone demanded.

"What kind of sand have you got?" I asked impatiently.

"Lady, I got every kinda sand in the book. Coarse-grain, medium-grain, fine-grain, scented, unscented, with pebbles, no pebbles, with sea shells, standard or deluxe, white sand, pink sand, black sand, custom-color sand, quicksand . . ."

"You have quicksand?" I asked incredulously.

"Lady, whaddaya think I am, Lawrence of Arabia? It's *like* quicksand. Ya wanna get stuck in the sand? I'm your man!"

"I don't want to get stuck in the sand!" I said, exasperated.

"Okay, lady. Well, when you figure out what kinda sand you want, give me a call!" he said and slammed down the phone.

I glanced in frustration at Anna and Richard. Putting Anna in preschool was supposed to give me time to work. But when I factored in drop-off and pickup time, lunch-prep time, researching show-and-tells, and rounding up school supplies, to say nothing of the time squandered arguing with surly sand vendors, the net gain in my workday seemed negligible.

In addition to which, the events of the previous night were now causing a definitive net loss in my readily available self-esteem, accompanied by a significant net gain in my paranoia. At school, I was now probably known as the tent lady—the woman responsible for the single greatest catastrophe ever to befall a Metropolitan social event. As far as Kim was concerned, in fact, I must have been the homicidal tent lady. And I worried that my pariah status would make Anna suspect number one in the gruesome murder of a hamster.

"Nonsense!" Bronwyn had said on the phone when she called this morning to find out why I hadn't shown up at drop-off. "Everyone knows it's not your fault. Kim *provoked* you. Anyway, that tent manufacturer ought to be sued!"

"I wish I could convince Kim that I wasn't trying to attack her," I said. I still remembered the look of terror on Kim's face as she saw me flying toward her.

"Oh, I wouldn't bother. She only cares about herself," Bronwyn said. "You know, I'm picking up some p.r.e.t.t.y. shocking information on her. I'll tell you everything when you come over for dinner tomorrow night. We need to plot strategy."

Dominique had also called to let me know she was in my camp. Of course, she seemed more interested in the drama of my situation than anything else. But at least she was talking to me.

Anna seemed to understand my predicament, because she immediately set about making it worse. While Richard, who had moved on from grading papers to reading one of his books, pretended to play with her with his feet, she was systematically embedding bits of egg into the carpet.

"Anna!" I said firmly. "Why are you making such a mess?"

"Because I want your attention," replied my emotionally precocious daughter.

"But you have Daddy's attention." I fumed, glaring at Richard.

"I don't want Daddy's attention. I want *your* attention!"

"You have my attention. Just don't make a mess!"

"But if I don't make a mess, I don't get your attention!"

She scurried back over to me, trailing little blobs of pork fat along the way.

"Richard!" I looked pleadingly at my husband. "I've got to work!"

"Well, I do, too!" he snapped back. "You know that if I don't publish my article on the Leeuwenhoek-Vermeer relationship this year, I'll never get promoted to principal assistant secretary of the Huygens Society!"

He pulled out one of his notebooks and lay back on the couch, giving up any pretense of childcare. "Besides," he added, "it was your idea to keep Anna home from school today."

"Why is it always *my* fault?" I said. "You could have taken her to school. Besides, how was I supposed to face those people after I brought the tent down on them?"

"Well, it was your idea to bring the tent down on them."

"My idea? I told you, I was trying to save—"

"Oh, all right," he interrupted. "It was an accident. So what? It's just a preschool. Why should we care what those silly people think? After we get through this year, we should just send her to the good old local public school, for God's sake. I'm sure it's perfectly okay."

Before Anna had been awarded the Forsythe Scholarship at Metropolitan, Richard's cavalier attitude toward her educational future had felt reassuring, a reality check that put everything in perspective. Now, however, this kind of comment felt like fingernails on a chalkboard. Richard always took the stance that he was above life's petty concerns. But I was starting to think he was infuriatingly out of touch.

"How do you know it's fine?" I asked him. "I've heard a lot of horror stories about our good old local public school. . . ."

"From whom, selfish and narrow-minded arrivistes who don't want their kids in a classroom with too many children of color?" he retorted.

". . . about overcrowded classrooms . . ." I fumed.

"Whatever."

". . . where they call on kids by serial number . . ."

"What?"

". . . and kids get constipated because the bathrooms are so disgusting!"

Richard was quiet for a moment. "Look, how about if I start taking Anna to Metropolitan?" he proposed, suddenly switching to the higher-ground approach.

"That would be fantastic!" I said. For a moment, I was pleased. Then my mind was overtaken by a suspicious thought.

"Why do you want to take her to school all of a sudden?" I asked.

"I think it'll help with . . . uh . . . separation . . ." Richard said weakly.

Suspicion confirmed.

"You just want to run into Amy!" I replied.

"No, I don't!" he said hotly.

"You want to impress her with what a great, involved father you are."

"You are impossible," he said. "You whine when I do nothing. Then when I want to help out, you whine even more. I can't win."

"That's not true!" I said. "This has nothing to do with helping me out. You just want to see your ex-girlfriend."

"Well, why shouldn't I see her from time to time?" he shot back. "You still talk to Len."

"Big deal," I fumed. "So I call Len twice a year. We've been friends for a lot longer than we were a couple. We broke up seven years ago."

"More like once a month!" he said. "I've got the long-distance bills to prove it!"

I felt a sudden stab of guilt but furiously rationalized it away. "It's totally different," I insisted, shaking my head.

"It's *not* different. It's the same," he said.

"No it *isn't,*" I said loudly. "I don't flirt with Len. He has a new girlfriend, some twenty-two-year-old makeup artist named Brandi, and *I'm happy for him*! Second of all, *Len* lives in *Los Angeles*! *Amy* lives on *Chambers Street*!"

"Look," he said, "Amy needs a friend. She's going through a tough time."

"Oh, really," I said sarcastically. "What, is she having trouble with her husband or something?"

"Actually, yes," he said, crossing his arms.

"Richard! Don't you see what she's doing?"

"No! I don't!" he shouted. "Don't you see how paranoid you're sounding?"

"I'm not paranoid! You're attacking me!"

"Now you're sounding like James. . . ."

"Leave my brother out of this!"

We were now in a double-jeopardy round. Bringing up my brother's troubles was even more dangerous than reopening the debate about Anna's name. But Richard always did when he really wanted to get me. I started to frantically search for my keys. I had to get out of there fast. I found them under a stack of yesterday's newspapers and marched to the door.

Suddenly, I heard a sobbing sound. I looked down. It was my daughter. Her tiny elbows jutted out on either side of her head, her hands held hard over her ears. Her eyes were squeezed shut, but tears were still falling from the corners. Her little face was contorted with anxiety and fear.

All at once, I saw myself in her place, cowering as my parents fought. I remembered the day my dad came home with a new car. My mom had thought they were saving for the kids' college funds. James and I sat, helpless, as they tore each other apart, lacerating each other with their words. I remembered promising myself during my pregnancy that I would never let my child feel what I had felt—or what my brother had felt, which was so much worse.

And here I was.

I squatted in front of Anna and gathered her in my arms. "I'm so sorry, Sweet Pea," I pleaded. "We love you so much. We are just . . . discussing . . ."

"Stop it!" she said. "Stop *picussing*! You are not *behaving*! You are not . . ." She struggled for the words. "*Sharing.*"

Guilt spread over me like an oil stain. I realized how selfish Richard and I had been for fighting in front of her. I held her in my arms and stroked her soft hair. "You're right, Sweet Pea," I said, rocking her back and forth. "You know, Daddy and I love each other very much. Even when we fight." I gave my husband an imploring look, but he refused to acknowledge me and knelt on the other side of Anna. I reached my hand out to touch his arm. He flinched.

I carried Anna into her room. "Let's play with some toys," I said, trying my best to inject a note of cheer into my voice even as my heart was sinking. We started to line up little plastic animals for "animal school," Anna's current favorite game. She put the zebra, the koala, and the giraffe all in a row. "This one is the naughty one!" She picked up the giraffe and smashed it into the zebra. "She needs a time out!"

As Anna resolved her trauma by acting out scenes of animal conflict, I subtly steered her toward a comfortable resolution. But as soon as I was sure that normalcy was sufficiently restored to my daughter's world, the free part of my mind began to return obsessively to the moments just before the tent fell on the rooftop of Emilio and Pilar's place.

I pictured the Metropolitan parents, their affluent, attractive faces turned to me with curiosity and mistrust. I pictured the pole slipping slowly from its place. And I pictured Jeffrey Forsythe standing at the center of the crowd. But in my mind, instead of wearing a suit, he was sitting in a boat on a secluded Caribbean cove, unclothed from the waist up, his muscled chest flexing as he hefted the oars. And I was sitting opposite him on the boat, feeling the hot sun and an even stronger heat from his eyes. . . .

I felt a strange sensation pass over me, like a slight shift in gravity. It was shocking and disorienting. My body suddenly felt unfamiliar. I shook my head as though trying to shake the image from my mind. Was I really having such absurd fantasies? And wholly unrelated to The Container Store? Me, a happily married woman! *Most of the time, at least,* I reminded myself. At the moment I was annoyed with Richard, but I knew the feeling would pass. In my heart, I knew I was just mentally getting revenge. I told myself it was a harmless diversion.

I shuffled the toy animals around in front of Anna. She now seemed to have entirely forgotten about our fight, but I worried that she had filed it away in some corner of her psyche, from which it would be exhumed years later by a psychotherapist, who would advise her to cut off all contact with her mother. Maybe I was the one who needed help with separation.

Richard entered the room tentatively. He picked up the giraffe and started to tell Anna why it had such a long neck. Anna became absorbed in his tale, and I gave him a grudging nod of thanks.

When the conversation had evolved into a happy but zoologi-

cally misleading story about the relationship between a daddy giraffe and his baby, I slid back to my "office" and returned to the
Sun & Frolic campaign.

"Sun and Frolic—where family stress just evaporates in the
warm Caribbean air."

"We provide the Sun, all you have to do is Frolic!"

It was hopeless. I'd never get the job done on time.

The phone rang. I reached to pick it up, preparing myself to
give the surly sand man a good tongue-lashing.

"Hey, Laura!" It was the cheerful voice of Carter, my boss. "I
was going to send you an e-mail, but then I thought, *What the hell?*
What's wrong with the old voice technology? So, anyway, I just
wanted to know how you're doing on the Sun and Frolic
piece. . . ."

Chapter 6

Polly put the kettle on, Polly put the kettle on
Polly put the kettle on, we'll all have tea.

"What's next?" Bronwyn said. "Cranberries!"

She tabbed her finger down the open page of her cookbook. "One-fourth cup."

I hunted around for measuring cups on the aircraft carrier–sized stainless-steel countertop that divided the kitchen from the vast open living space of her loft. It was clear that Bronwyn's invitation to dinner was part of her attempt to soften my humiliation at having brought down the tent at the Metropolitan party two nights before, and that she was going the extra mile by doing some of the cooking herself. I determined that I would make it up to her somehow.

I found a half-cup measure and filled it halfway with dried cranberries.

"Oh, let me help you," Bronwyn said, smiling sympathetically.

She opened and closed several cabinet doors. "Now, where did Maria hide them?" she asked herself before locating a quarter-cup measure with a triumphant "Aha!"

As she handed it to me, it slipped out of my grasp and clanged loudly on the counter. "I am such a klutz!" I moaned, putting my head in my hands.

"Oh, sweetie," Bronwyn said gently for the twentieth time, picking up the measuring cup and filling it with dried cranberries. "We know it wasn't your fault. Emilio is totally fine with it. In fact, he thinks it was kind of funny."

"What about Pilar?" I asked.

"She's going to take a little more time," Bronwyn said, scrunching her face into a grimace. "Maybe the tent pole knocked her implants out of line."

I grinned in spite of myself.

"Anyway," she continued, "I have some very interesting information about our *friend*."

"What?" I knew she was referring to Kim.

"You're gonna love this," she said. "But let's open the wine first."

From the oven came the warm, reassuring smell of a roasting chicken. Bronwyn's housekeeper, Maria, had prepared it and put it in to bake before we arrived. Our contribution to the meal was a precision-engineered Martha Stewart Alpine Forest Salad. Bronwyn placed each ingredient in an ebony serving bowl with a delicately filigreed silver rim. It was exquisite. I was proud of the cheery kitchen stuff Richard and I had acquired at Crate & Barrel, but this was in a completely different category.

"A wedding present," Bronwyn explained, as though reading my mind.

Bronwyn and Lloyd had been married for six years, but to judge from their Worth Street loft, it seemed like the wedding had taken place only last week. Hanging on the walls and resting on the shelves of various handcrafted walnut bookcases were dozens of photographs of the grand event. There was Bronwyn, posing in front of Saint Patrick's Cathedral on Fifth Avenue in her sleek white gown, her hair back in a loose knot with wispy tendrils floating around her face. In heels, she was slightly taller than her husband. Lloyd had sandy hair and large features that seemed to disappear into his meaty mug, but his green eyes wore an expression of pride and affection that made him look gallant, if not exactly handsome.

"Are these your parents?" I indicated a picture on the mantelpiece of the bride seated next to an elegant, white-haired couple. She nodded.

"Lloyd's mom?" I said, pointing to a picture of the groom standing next to a large, frizzy-haired woman.

Bronwyn nodded again. "Lloyd was raised by his mom. He never talks about his dad. It was one of those situations where the father lives at the bar and forgets his kids' names. For a while, Lloyd's mom worked the night shift at a 7-Eleven. They lived in the boondocks in Maryland. His birth name was Floyd, but after high school he won a full academic scholarship to the University of Pennsylvania and renamed himself Lloyd."

She paused. "I have so much respect for him. Coming from a place like that and creating all of this . . ." Bronwyn gestured to the space around her.

She began to tell me the story of how they had first met, at the bank where he was a partner and she worked in human resources. "Lloyd had just been profiled in the *Wall Street Journal* as one of the top young bankers in the city," she continued, chopping the fennel ferociously. "You wouldn't believe what women will do to get a guy like that. They came out of nowhere. Like mosquitoes on the Fourth of July or something!"

But Lloyd was smitten with Bronwyn the moment he laid eyes on her at the company Christmas party. "He pursued me pretty hard." She smiled a guilty, happy smile. "We tried to keep it secret. He was a big deal at work, you know, and we didn't want anyone accusing him of favoritism. So in order to avoid running into people on the street, we'd check into these amazing hotels for the weekend."

Bronwyn sighed. I looked at one of the wedding photos, a shot of her in her white silk dress posed between her two younger brothers—both freckled and coltish, with the same distinctive honey-colored eyes as their sister. They'd grown up in picture-perfect Stowe, Vermont. Bronwyn's father was a corporate attorney and her mother was active in the local Junior League. "My mom *worships* Lloyd," Bronwyn assured me. "She always says that Lloyd's and my wedding day was the happiest day of her life. My first husband and I got married at City Hall."

When the salad had been assembled, we moved over to the living room, where a pair of pale green leather sofas formed an island in the middle of the main floor. The walls were lined with landscape paintings, sculptures of vaguely organic forms, and other decorative artwork. Over the mock mantelpiece was a photo of an enormous orchid in soft focus.

Just as we sat down, Harrison's nanny, Bernadette, emerged from a separate children's wing that had been built into the back of the loft.

"How are my little pumpkins?" Bronwyn asked her.

As usual, Bronwyn had two nannies on duty—one for four-year-old Harrison, and another for two-year-old Tess.

"Fine. Tess is asleep, and Nadine is reading to Harrison," Bernadette replied, then hesitated.

"What is it, Bernadette?" Bronwyn asked.

"I need to take my mother to the doctor tomorrow morning," Bernadette said. "Can I come in at noon?"

A small crease briefly split Bronwyn's forehead, then quickly disappeared. "Sure." She smiled benevolently. "No problem."

Bernadette gathered her belongings and prepared to exit the apartment. I noticed that her jacket had been expertly patched at the collar.

Bronwyn walked over to the other side of the living room and stepped into an alcove that had discreetly and elegantly been out-fitted as an office, her feet clopping on the polished pale wood floor. She slid an Aeron office chair out from a desk and pulled out a hidden tray with a keyboard and mouse, and a huge flat screen on the wall came to life.

"Have you seen this, Laura?" she asked, beckoning me over. On-screen was a software version of a scheduling book, with each day broken down into an hour-by-hour grid.

"Lloyd got it from the office," she explained as she clicked open a window marked "Bernadette" and input some changes.

"I use this computer for school stuff, too," she added. "If you need to do something for the auction committee, you can come work here anytime."

"Look at this!" She popped open a window marked "Tess." Scanning it quickly, I could see that her two-year-old's week was booked solid: art appreciation, piano, tumbling, ballet. I felt a familiar stab of anxiety: Tess at two had a far more sophisticated schedule than Anna did at three and a half (or than I did at ten, for that matter).

It was one thing to know that most of Anna's classmates at Metropolitan spent their afternoons shuttling from one résumé-building class to another, while Anna had to make due with regular trips to the zoo or the museum or the children's hour at the local library. But it was another to see it rendered with all the power of Microsoft Office Tools for XP. I made a mental note to enroll Anna in something—*anything*.

"How does a two-year-old play the piano?" I asked.

Bronwyn laughed. "She doesn't, really. But they say it's good for training the ear. Besides, Rae Fishman is the best piano teacher in the city. Her wait list is a mile long, but a friend from Bloom got me in."

"And what does Tess do in art appreciation?" I pictured Anna at the Metropolitan Museum, gently slathering a Monet with scrambled eggs.

"They take her around to the galleries. You should see the journal she keeps for class. The instructor calls her a little Jackson Pollock!"

She accidentally clicked on a button marked "Harrison," then swiftly closed it and started opening up other windows in rapid succession. She was too fast for the computer and it crashed.

"Oh, *man!*" Bronwyn wailed, hitting the power button. She picked up the phone and punched in a number. Turning to me, she whispered, "Jared. My computer guy. He's the best."

"Hey," she said plaintively into the phone. "It's me!"

Pause. "Well, you know me. I turned it on and it exploded! Could you come over tomorrow morning? Maria will let you in. Great!"

Bronwyn rolled her office chair over to a large filing cabinet. "Let me see if I can find Tess's portfolio." She began sliding open the drawers, revealing a complex system of color-coded folders inside. "God, I should sell this stuff to the Parents League," she muttered. "You know, getting Harrison into preschool was my full-time job last year." She showed me her stash of intelligence on the private schools of Manhattan. Bronwyn had amassed a folder for each school, stuffed with applications, promotional materials, correspondence, and other odds and ends. Each folder was marked with a number indicating the desirability of the school. Metropolitan was marked "1," and it was the fattest of the bunch. Her filing system looked orderly from a distance, but glancing in the individual folders, I could see that in reality it was quite a mess.

We moved back to the living area and plopped onto one of the pale green sofas. I flipped through a coffee-table book on antique furniture.

"My decorator brought that for me to look at," she said, nodding toward my book. "For our house in East Hampton."

Bronwyn and Lloyd, I knew, had recently purchased a country house in Long Island's fabled new money preserve.

"It must be great to have a place to get away to on the weekends," I said only semi-enviously. I had always told myself that a country house just meant another place to clean.

"It is," Bronwyn said. "It's pretty new, but it's got an old, colonial feel to it. Sherry drove up to look at it with us. You know, she just decorated Heath Ledger's loft across the street.

"Anyway, I think I'm about ready for that wine, aren't you?" she continued, bringing out a bottle of Sancerre and pouring two glasses.

We sat in silence for a moment.

"So, what were you going to tell me about Kim?" I asked her. I was certain that news about our committee member had been one of Bronwyn's other motivations for inviting me to dinner.

"Wait! I think the chicken's done." Bronwyn marched into the kitchen and took the roaster out. It was perfectly browned, and the mouthwatering smell filled the apartment.

"By the way, did I ever tell you about the trick Kim tried to pull for Maura, one of her work buddies?" she said, pulling a thermometer out of the chicken.

"No," I said.

"So this woman, Maura, applied to Metropolitan last year. Kim was trying to get her in. I think they were involved in some shady quid pro quo—you know, you scratch my back, I help get your kid into preschool."

This wasn't as shocking as perhaps it should have been. It had long been obvious to me that private, informal deals such as these were more of a factor in preschool admissions than anyone wanted to admit.

"Anyway," Bronwyn continued, "Maura worked at Lloyd's

bank, and she claimed she was a senior partner. Which she was *not*. It was so creepy."

"Wow. So what happened?"

"She didn't get in, of course. Metropolitan has pretty high standards on that kind of thing. I mean, if the parents are lying on their application forms, they are *not* the kind of people you want to be associating with. So I had to tell Sunny. It wouldn't have been ethical to allow Maura to mislead the school."

I thought Bronwyn had chosen to meddle more than I would have wanted to, if only because I couldn't afford the risk. But I just nodded.

"So what's up with Kim now?" I asked.

"Okay, so I checked with Bernadette," she said, taking a seat next to me on the sofa. "You know, she's picked up some pretty interesting details. It turns out that every Tuesday and Thursday after school, Kim's nanny collects Jake from school and drops him off with his mother at the Starbucks on the corner of Twenty-seventh and First."

She looked at me meaningfully.

"Twenty-seventh and First . . ." I said, trying to figure out what that would mean.

"Exactly! You wouldn't know about it unless your kid has problems. But Anna isn't the kind of girl who needs professional help, is she?" She laughed.

"No!" I blurted out. Of course, it wasn't quite true—I had in fact taken Anna to therapy at the height of her "regressive" phase. But with the mystery of Snowflake's murder still unsolved, I wasn't ready to tell Bronwyn about that.

"So that got me thinking. I called our friend Dan. He's the best psychologist in the city. I asked, if you had a kid like Jake, and you couldn't treat him yourself, where would you take him?"

"Where?"

"Bellevue Hospital, Pediatric Psychiatry!"

"On Twenty-seventh and First!"

"Exactly!"

"No way!"

"Yes way!"

We both took another sip of the Sancerre. I tried to picture Jake sneaking up to the hamster cage and silently twisting Snowflake's neck. I had probably seen Jake nearly every weekday at the school drop-off. I had never seen his father but had concluded that Kim was married to a white guy. Jake's straight, fine hair had a reddish cast, and his almond-shaped eyes were paler than those of his mother. It was hard to picture him doing something so evil. Then again, he did seem kind of aloof. And even Ted Bundy must have been a cute kid. I shuddered.

"I actually feel sorry for Jake," Bronwyn said. "Kids don't go around whacking hamsters unless they've got major issues."

"He needs attention," I said, nodding in agreement.

"Yeah, well, he's not going to get it from her."

Bronwyn looked at me even more meaningfully. "And now that she's going around telling everyone you attacked her at the party, she's convinced she's going to be able to pin the blame on Anna."

I put my head in my hands again. So it was true. As far as the parents of Metropolitan knew, I was a social misfit who had passed on some inherited form of dementia to her undeserving scholarship brat. In my head, I could still hear the screams in the darkness under the collapsed tent.

I repeated to myself the mantra that it was just a school, just a hamster, that we would be fine. But it wasn't working. Just several weeks ago, I had started the school year feeling confident about my ability to keep my feet on the ground in the social vortex of Metropolitan. My position on the auction committee had seemed to indicate smooth roads ahead. Now I was starting to feel that the terrain was unsteady and unpredictable.

"I think Kim is trying to win over Jeffrey," Bronwyn finally said. "I know she's pushing some angle to get favors from the school."

Suddenly, I remembered the conversation I'd overheard at the party.

"I heard them agree to meet at the Hotel Gansevoort—Wednesday at eleven a.m.," I volunteered. "I wonder what that's about?"

We digested the information for a few moments.

"Oh my God!" Bronwyn shot out of her seat and started pacing the room, a look of sheer disgust on her face.

"What?"

"You don't think that Jeffrey and Kim are having an affair?"

We'd both had the same thought at the same time. I tried to picture Jeffrey and Kim making out. I couldn't see it. Jeffrey's wife, Eve, had such a soft appeal, while Kim was so businesslike. But then I remembered the way Jeffrey had looked at me at the party. Clearly, his radar was turned on. So much had happened that night, I hadn't had a chance to ponder the implications. Now I did. I had to admit a stab of annoyance that it wasn't only me he found attractive, and that he might simply in fact be an indiscriminate flirt.

"Nah," I said nervously.

"Maybe you're right," Bronwyn said doubtfully. "She's such a cold fish."

We sat in silence. I thought again about Kim and Jeffrey cavorting at the Gansevoort. What would they do? Order up the yellowtail carpaccio and then lick it off each other? I was starting to feel little stings of jealousy.

The thought of carpaccio reminded me that I was very hungry.

"Speaking of fish . . ." I started to say.

Suddenly, the door to the apartment swung open.

"Hi, honey." It was Lloyd. He appeared to be a bit older than he looked in his wedding photos in a way that couldn't be attributed to the mere passage of time. His sandy hair was thinning at the top and his green eyes looked weary. But his well-fitting suit and polished wingtips gave him an appealing, slightly dandified air.

Bronwyn quickly got up to greet him. "Hi, babes," she said, putting on a sunny smile. She looked slightly dazed. As he hung up his coat, they gave each other a pursed-lipped peck on the mouth.

"How was your trip?" she asked.

"Great," he replied.

She introduced me as a Metropolitanite.

"Great!" he said, giving me a firm handshake as though I was a business client. "How do you like the school?"

"Great!" I replied without thinking.

"We were just talking about school now," Bronwyn said.

He nodded. "Metropolitan has a *great* reputation."

We sat down at the table. Lloyd told us about the highlights of his three days in Chicago on business. Bronwyn chatted about the furniture in their Hamptons country home while carefully picking all the cranberries out of her salad. Lloyd wolfed down the chicken amiably.

"Good stuff, honey," he said to Bronwyn from across the table. "So, how are the kids?"

"Harrison is *obsessed* with soccer," she replied. "And Tess has really taken to Nadine." She smiled.

"We caught our last nanny stealing," she said, turning to me. "Nadine's new. She's from Martinique, and she's even teaching Tess some French. Now, when you ask Tess in French what sound a dog makes, she goes, *"wouaf, wouaf."*

Lloyd took another bite of his chicken. "Just make sure she's not learning any of that gutter French."

"Of course not, honey," Bronwyn replied with a slightly embarrassed smile, then awkwardly changed the subject.

"You know, this school thing is getting a little tricky."

"How's that, honey?" he asked.

"Oh, you know," said Bronwyn, shaking her head. "Some of these class mothers will do anything to get ahead."

"Well, just let me know if I can help," Lloyd replied.

It was beginning to seem as though Lloyd had prepared for family life by modeling himself on sitcom dads of the *Bewitched* era. Then, remembering Bronwyn's kindness, I scolded myself: *He* was being perfectly pleasant. Maybe *I* was just a conversation snob. Richard and I certainly had our ups and downs, but at least we both always had plenty to say to each other and enjoyed saying it, perhaps to a fault. By comparison, the conversation between Bronwyn and Lloyd felt weirdly constrained, as though they were two people at a bus stop. However, given what Richard and I had been saying to each other on the day of our fight, I suddenly saw that this approach might have some advantages.

As we peacefully finished off the meal, I made a private vow to spend more of the rare "grown-up time" Richard and I occasionally managed to find discussing things like the weather or the subtleties of alternate-side-of-the-street parking regulations. This vision of a serene, if boring, marital heaven was interrupted by Harrison's voice, suddenly piping in from the other end of the living room.

"Mommy, look!" he said proudly, appearing at the doorway in cotton cowboy pajamas. He wore the same mischievous look I had seen at Serena's birthday party. "Am I being fancy?" Somehow, he'd escaped from the nanny and had smeared the area around his mouth with a fuchsia Chanel lipstick, which he was now waving around as if it were a pointy-point.

"Oh my God!" Bronwyn shrieked. She rose from the table abruptly and rushed over to the boy with a napkin in her hand and began rubbing his face furiously.

Lloyd's mild manners fell away as he stood up ramrod-straight at the table, almost knocking over his chair, and shouted across the room, "Harrison, you are *a very naughty boy!*"

Nadine, who looked as though she had been caught dozing, appeared and started making cautious fussing noises over Harrison.

Ignoring everyone, Bronwyn strode over, bundled up her squirming and by now howling son, and carried him out of the room with Nadine following anxiously behind. On the way out, Bronwyn turned and, changing seamlessly to a conversational tone, said to me, "Relax, Laura. I'll be back in a minute."

From the other room, I heard the sound of water being turned on and Bronwyn's angry chastisements.

Lloyd sat down and smiled at me as if he were returning to the table after a regrettably urgent caller had provoked him to breach the laws of etiquette by leaving it. "Kids," he said with a friendly shrug, breaking off the end of a baguette and taking a bite.

We sat without speaking. The only sounds were of Lloyd's chewing and Harrison's muffled, distant sobbing. I began to reappraise the virtues of making impeccably good manners such a priority. Lloyd had been gone for three days, and he couldn't give his kid a hug? Anna had done much worse than play with makeup in her bids for attention. I wanted to go into the bathroom and comfort Harrison, but I knew better than to interfere. Things were starting to feel a little tense.

"So . . . do you travel a lot on business?" I asked, trying to make conversation. I still wasn't entirely sure what he did.

"Sometimes," Lloyd said. This didn't leave any obvious room for rejoinder, and I was relieved when I heard the bathroom door open and glimpsed Bronwyn ushering her son into his bedroom. Then she returned to the kitchen and opened the refrigerator.

"We're out of milk," she announced a little too cheerfully. "Bernadette must have forgotten to pick it up. I'm going to have to go out and get milk for Harry."

"I'll walk out with you," I said to her. I got up and began to gather my things.

"Honey, I'll get the milk," Lloyd said.

"No, I'll go," Bronwyn replied quickly.

"No, really, I don't mind," Lloyd said, rising quickly from the table. For the first time, I wondered if he was smiling at her or clenching his teeth.

I piped up, "I could get the milk."

"Don't be silly, you're our guest," Bronwyn said reflexively. Her eyes seemed to be a bit too bright, and she blinked a few times.

"Yeah, don't worry about it," Lloyd said, sitting back down at the table. Nobody spoke. We seemed to have reached an impasse of social correctness. Suddenly, the room felt too warm.

"Okay, well, I should get home," I said, standing up and moving toward my purse. Bronwyn started to clear the table with a fixed smile on her face as Lloyd intercepted me at the closet and solicitously helped me on with my coat. The awkward moment seemed to have passed.

"Great to meet you, Laura," Lloyd said, reaching out and shaking my hand again.

"Thanks so much for coming over!" Bronwyn said brightly, the smile still pinned to her face. "Let's talk tomorrow." She put her hand into the shape of a phone. "We need to make a plan."

When I arrived home at 9:30 p.m., Anna was wide awake and bouncing on the bed at Richard's encouragement. "Mommy, look," she said gleefully. "I'm a cat-cow who jumps. Cat-cows are good jumpers."

I shook my head, exasperated but secretly pleased by this familiar and comforting lawlessness. "It's *way* past her bedtime, Richard. How am I going to get her up in time for school?"

"Uh, she was having difficulty getting to sleep," he said sheepishly. My goodwill evaporated and I narrowed my eyes. Something was out of place.

I glanced at the floor by the bed and saw a toy I'd never seen in our house before. It was a delicate, antiquey doll in nineteenth-century farm-girl dress. It looked expensive.

"What's this?" I picked it up.

"Oh, well, uh, that must be Anna's. . . ." he said awkwardly.

"It's not Anna's," I corrected him.

"No, I mean the other Anna. . . ."

"What? *Amy was here?*"

The suspicion that Richard and his ex-girlfriend had conspired to present an alibi about the "Anna" issue behind my back at the rooftop party returned in full force. Now I wondered if they had been sharing a laugh at my expense over the tent fiasco.

"She just came to say hello!" Richard said.

"You invited your ex-girlfriend over without telling me?"

"No! She called because she wanted to set up a playdate! So I just said why don't you—"

"I can't believe you let that ugly troll into our house!" I exclaimed.

"What do you have against her?" he said. "I mean, it's not like she's wasting any time thinking about you. She didn't even mention your name."

"That's exactly my point!" I said. "She wants to undermine me! She's an *underminer!*"

He shook his head in disgust. "You should hear yourself, Laura! You are so paranoid! She's a perfectly nice person. You know what I think? I think you're jealous."

I was jealous. But I was also right.

"Just get out! Leave us alone!" I furiously pushed my husband out of Anna's room. I slammed the door shut and threw myself on the bed.

As I lay there in an incoherent fury, my daughter climbed up beside me.

"But Mommy, Anna and I had fun," Anna said seriously. "I showed her how to play cat-cow. Besides, Anna's mother isn't *ug-guley*. She is *very* pretty."

Chapter 7

Pussycat, pussycat, where have you been?
I've been to London to look at the Queen

The line of silver SUVs gleamed in the morning sun like a bullet train. Doors crunched open and shut, disgorging an army of tots in cashmere sweaters and woolen pinafores. Along the sidewalk, a host of strollers converged on the same destination. Nannies wearing bored expressions dropped their charges off at the door with little ceremony. The daddies often didn't even make it that far. They tossed their kids up the steps like footballs and then ran off, clutching briefcases. Mothers lingered in their Prada flats and Burberry jackets, engaging in coochie-coo good-bye rituals.

I had never really felt at ease during drop-off at Metropolitan. Ever since Anna's birth, I hadn't been much of a snappy dresser, and certainly never before lunch. And yet Metropolitan moms made it look effortless. When I was around them, I always felt like nothing fit quite right and my hair was a mess. Of course,

now, with the party fiasco fresh in everybody's mind, I felt posi-
tively radioactive.

To make things worse, Anna was in a feisty mood. The way she
clung to my legs told me that separation was not going to go well
today.

I bent over and tried to pry her little fingers from my thigh.
Out of the corner of my eye, I saw Pilar stepping out of the backseat of her chauffeured, monster-sized SUV, followed by her little boy, who looked around him as if he already knew that his
great-grandfather had been a Cuban count. Pilar, who was sport-
ing stiletto heels, low-cut jeans, and a cropped top that revealed
at least four inches of her tanned midriff, pretended not to see
me. I spotted Serena's mother, dressed today in a kick-pleated
skirt and a blouse with a large bow, but as our eyes met she
quickly and ostentatiously busied herself with unbuttoning her
daughter's cardigan.

Anna turned her little face up to mine.

"Mommy, where is *our* driver?" she asked in her small, high voice.

"Sweet Pea, we don't have a car," I said, trying to keep my voice
even. "So we don't need a driver!"

Pilar let slip the hint of a smirk.

"Mommy, cat-cows don't like school," Anna said to me.

I saw the other women's eyes dart in our direction.

"Sweet Pea, big girls have fun at school," I said. "At school they
can play with their friends."

"I am not a big girl." Anna stomped. "I am a cat-cow. A cat-cow
baby."

I sighed. I had seen other children burst into tears at drop-off, but so far Anna's "transition period" had been pretty uneventful. Now it looked as though my good luck on this front might have come to an end.

"Cat-cow mommies are allowed to go to school with their babies," she said to me as we entered her classroom. "They can go to school all day long."

"That's great," I said, "but at our school, mommies aren't allowed."

Anna's little lower lip started to quiver, and her face started to flush. I hugged her tight, but she collapsed in my arms and crumpled to the floor.

"I'm a baby! Carry me!" Anna said plaintively, curling her body into a ball.

"Sweet Pea." I tried to lift her gently by her arms. She was dead weight.

The other moms pretended to go about their business. But I knew what they were thinking: *Canopy vandal! Wearer of all black! No wonder her daughter can't control herself!*

I had a vision of Anna as a lonely and defeated third-grader, shivering in a thin sleeping bag under the forest skies in a ring of stones while the other Girl Scouts snuggled up safe in their firmly supported tents.

I glanced around for help and saw Tori, who was standing in the middle of the classroom, looking on dumbly, seemingly unable to grasp that my daughter's entire camping future was at stake. Finally, I manipulated us within her reach.

"Anna, it's your turn to water the plants," I said loudly. "Tori's going to give you the watering can." I smiled cheerily and pointed at the watering can, shooting Tori an urgent look, which she finally seemed to understand.

"Oh, yes, Anna," she said, grasping the watering can and holding it out to Anna. "It's your turn today." Anna took the can, and I gave Tori a grateful nod before sneaking out of the room.

With Anna momentarily back on the right social development track, and feeling the distinctive combination of relief and separation pangs that I felt whenever I had some time to myself, I turned to look for Sunny. I had considered letting Richard face drop-off, but then remembered that, at Bronwyn's urging, I had signed up to help accompany prospective parents on the Metropolitan school tour, and that today was the day I was scheduled to report for duty. Looking around cautiously, I caught sight of Dominique near the children's cubbies, attired in a flared skirt and fur stole, dropping off her daughter, Emmy.

"Laura, you are here today!" Dominique, making expansive continental gestures as she approached, greeted me with an extravagant kiss on both cheeks as her daughter skipped off into the classroom. "Are you okay? You know everybody is still talking about that party!"

Her intentions were probably good, but she seemed to be speaking for the little old deaf lady in the last row of the uppermost balcony of the Metropolitan Opera House. I winced.

"I'm fine," I said, dodging her theatrically sympathetic look.

"But, I mean, Laura, that was *really* . . ."

"I know, I'm trying to forget about it."

I made a quick decision to trust her. After all, she had called to console me about the party, and anyway, she was the only ally available.

"Listen, Dominique, there's something I have to tell you," I said with as much spy-movie finesse as I could muster. Taking her with me into the hallway, I whispered what I had learned at Bronwyn's house about Kim's secret visits to the pediatric ward. Dominique's eyes darted excitedly around as she listened. Then I mentioned the mysterious appointment with Jeffrey at the Gansevoort.

"Really?" she said, her voice rich with the thrill of intrigue. Her eyes lit up and her face came alive. "Jeffrey? How amazing! And she is not so very attractive!"

"You don't really think they're having an affair or anything?"

"Oh, don't be so American!" she chided me. "Of course they are having an affair! *Mais oui!* Why else would they meet at that hotel? He is a very good-looking man, and he is probably bored with Eve. When you have been married for so many years, it is inevitable. Do not be so naïve! For most of us, making love to the person we married becomes as exciting as shaving your legs. Kim, she has that appeal of the *exotique*."

"Maybe," I replied doubtfully.

"Laura, this is incredible! We must *do* something!"

Before I could answer, Sunny suddenly emerged from one of the classrooms in a magenta suit, a pair of reading spectacles joining the opal on her bosom. "Are we ready for the tour?" she asked me brightly. "After that, you and I can talk!"

Dominique again kissed me on both cheeks, made the universal signal for "call me," and left the building.

* * *

The Metropolitan Preschool tour was a very significant part of the admissions process. For those who weren't celebrities or didn't have an insider pulling strings for them, it was often their "performance" on the tour that decided their child's educational future.

"It'll be good for you, Laura," Bronwyn had advised soberly. "The more you can help out the school . . ." She left the rest of the sentence unspoken. "Besides," she added, "now that we've completed the process and placed our kids at Metropolitan, it's nice to give back."

Now, her face beaming, Sunny ushered me into the front lobby, where we gathered up a pair of couples. "Ladies, gentlemen, it's wonderful to welcome you to Metropolitan! Thank you for taking time out of your busy schedules to visit us here today. I know that you will all want to get back to your responsibilities as soon as you can."

At the sound of her cheery voice, a hush descended over the group. The applicants greeted her with the nervous enthusiasm of job-seekers. One of the women was wearing a mauve twinset, her sleek hair pulled back in a demure ponytail. Her husband, handsome and spectacled, wore a dark gray suit. The other woman, a plump brunette in a frilly blouse, had clearly spent the morning in a salon—the kind that uses too much hair spray. Her husband had slicked back his own hair with some kind of grease, and was dressed in a rumpled pair of trousers and a plaid sweater.

I followed Sunny, and she led the cooperative group through

the facilities. There was the music room where children met once a week to sing Peter, Paul, and Mary tunes around a grand piano. The library was stocked with picture books maintained in neat alphabetical order and topical arrangements by the parent library volunteers. The theater room had a puppet stage in one corner and was well equipped with costumes and dress-up clothes. Sunny took us to the basement to see the gym, a fluorescent-lit space with some large rubber balls and floor mats. And then we peeked in on the classrooms, where groups of children were engaged in various activities. The construction-papered walls had been decorated with materials from class projects about the four seasons and farm animals.

One of the classrooms had a clear window installed next to the door, facilitating observation. "Let's stop here and watch for a few moments," Sunny said beneficently. The children wore plastic smocks over their clothes and daubed watercolors with long-handled paintbrushes at various low tables scattered about the room. I was startled to notice Pilar, who had evidently volunteered that day as a "class mother," or teacher's assistant. She was still wearing her stilettos, and she tottered around the classroom giddily, cooing over one child and patting another on the head like Glinda the Good Witch granting blessings to her colony of Munchkins.

"The children in Classroom Two are painting pictures of their country houses," Sunny said. She nodded politely in the direction of Pilar. "Each parent has the opportunity to sign up as class mother for her child's class as often as she wants. At Metropolitan, we encourage that level of detailed parental involvement and community-building. Virtually every mother—and father, of course"—she nodded to the men in the group—"is moved to involve him- or herself in a deeper way at our school." She flashed a smile.

I hadn't signed up yet as a "class mother," mainly because I was already busy with the auction committee. I needed more time to work as it was. But in Anna's class, there never seemed to be a shortage of mothers willing to volunteer. Several of them had confided to me that during the applications process, they had "marketed" themselves to Metropolitan and the other private schools as stay-at-home moms who were eager to donate their time. It seemed a little warped, as it put the offspring of women with successful careers at a bizarre disadvantage. But frankly, I wasn't sure Tori and the other assistant teacher would have been able to handle the class without the extra help. And anyway, it was technically voluntary.

We watched in respectful silence as Pilar cooed words of encouragement to the children, adjusting the smock on one or showing another how to hold a paintbrush. After a few moments, she ambled over to a low table near the door where we came in and reached down to pick up a fresh tray of paintbrushes. With all eyes on her, she bent over slowly from the hips. Her cropped top, loose around the neck, fell away from her body, giving us all an unobstructed view of her breasts—braless, as we could all see. Pilar held her position for a dozen-odd beats. Then she straightened up slowly, flashed us all a giddy smile, and sashayed back to the children with her tray. I glanced at the other parents. Mouths had dropped open, and one of the papas cleared his throat. Even Sunny seemed momentarily at a loss for words.

"Uh, let's move along to Classroom Three," she said, regaining her composure, herding us down the hall to a room full of four-year-olds who were sitting quietly in a circle. Inside, the class mother, a woman in her mid-forties with short, curly hair, was demonstrating how to make Play-Doh from scratch. We again watched silently for a few minutes, observing the pleasantly ordered scene. I had a feeling I wasn't the only one having a hard time forgetting Pilar's strangely timed exhibitionism. I didn't remember the bespectacled husband as having had quite so much color in his cheeks when we were back in the lobby.

Finally, the tour was over. Sunny led us to the conference room off the main entryway. We sat around a table in a semicircle while Sunny offered a brief history of the school's approach to learning.

I had heard the story countless times already. Thirty years ago, a group of educators emerged from certain villages in northern Italy with a new philosophy of early-childhood education based on "community values," as Sunny explained, and "the importance of object-centered instruction." Frankly, I had never been able to discern how these ideas differed from the philosophies of other preschools. From my conversations at New York City parks, it seemed as though all preschool kids did the same stuff, more or less—reading, singing, art, free play, snack time. But apparently, Sunny was sold. And she certainly knew how to sell it.

"So that's it!" she concluded brightly, after hitting the high points. She clasped her hands. "Any questions?"

It was a critical moment for the prospective Metropolitanites.

The quality of the questions they asked was a crucial indicator of their suitability for the school.

"How do you deal with separation anxiety?" the lady with too much hair spray blurted out. *A bad start,* I thought. Didn't she know that private schools took a dim view of children who do not separate well?

"Good question!" Sunny responded. "In the beginning of the school year, we observe a three-week transition period where children attend school in increasing time increments. Keep in mind that the week before school begins, the teachers visit each child at home in his or her loft or town house. That creates a level of familiarity, which the children find reassuring."

I thought back on my own experience with Metropolitan's pre-preschool ritual. When Tori had come to visit us the week before school began, she hadn't said a word. She had just perched on one of our kitchen chairs, looking young and scared. Maybe the home visits had been helpful to some of the other kids. But in our case, it hadn't seemed to make much of a difference.

"Any other questions?" Sunny looked pointedly at the other couple.

"What opportunities do parents have for getting involved in the school . . . in addition to volunteering as class mother?" Mauve Twinset asked, fixing a reverent gaze on Sunny.

Slam dunk, I thought.

"Well!" Sunny said heartily. "I'm glad you asked. Our parent body is passionate about early childhood education." She indicated a row of family photographs on the wall under a discreet label that read "Friends of Metropolitan."

"Friends of Metropolitan organize dinner parties and other events. Three times a year, different families volunteer their country homes and estates as places to meet for weekend retreats. That way, they can discuss school business in a relaxed environment. Of course," Sunny added, nodding at me, "parents who are . . . *not in a position* . . . to become Friends of Metropolitan are not excluded from offering meaningful contributions to the school. Laura, for instance, is on our auction committee. . . ."

At this, Mauve Twinset focused her expertly mascara-ed eyes on me like high-beams.

"That sounds like fun!" she said sweetly. "I have heard such great things about Metropolitan's annual auction." It crossed my mind that she had somehow already heard about the disaster on Emilio and Pilar's rooftop.

She looked back at Sunny, projecting the kind of naïvely fevered enthusiasm for the preschool that one usually associates with teenage crushes. Sunny smiled encouragingly. The other couple glanced at each other nervously.

"Well, I'll leave Laura to answer the rest of your questions," Sunny said. "It has been such a pleasure meeting you all." She shook hands with the parents and stood up, limping slightly as she exited the room.

After Sunny left, the couples stared at me uneasily.

"So, how challenging is the curriculum here?" the rumpled man asked abruptly. "I mean, our son is very, very smart. In fact, he's been accepted at Fisher."

Fisher was the notoriously competitive public elementary school for the "talented and gifted," the holy grail of New York's low- and middle-income families, and one of the few gifted public schools in the city with a pre-K program. Only kids who ranked in the top two percent of specially administered aptitude tests were even considered, and even then there was only a one-in-ten chance of admission. The quality of instruction was said to be competitive with that of the "top-tier" private schools—plus, it was free.

"That's amazing," Mauve Twinset breathed.

"Yeah," he said. "But then we hired a preschool consultant. She said if we have any interest in ever sending him to a private middle school or high school, we should forget about the public gifted program because 'nobody knows the school directors.' " He shrugged. "So, anyway, I'm just trying to figure it all out. . . ."

He stopped short. Under the desk, I saw his wife extracting her high heel from his foot. "We're not figuring it out, we know what we want," she said almost pleadingly. "We want our son to go to Metropolitan."

Looking at them, I wished I could reassure them that their son would be accepted and that Metropolitan was indeed a superior program to any other. But then I wondered, *What makes me so sure the school is that good?* I really didn't have anything to compare it to.

"Well, we're not even considering any of the public schools," Mauve Twinset said to me, very just-us-girls. "By the way," she added conspiratorially, "didn't I see you at Bloom the other day? You know, I've been a member since my second trimester!"

After peppering me with a few more questions, the parents eventually made their way out. I walked through the halls and over to the headmistress's office.

Sunny was poring over some papers on her desk, but when I

knocked on her open door, she swiveled her chair around. "Come in!" she said, giving me a big smile.

I took a seat on the L-shaped sofa against the wall and inspected a museum poster of Van Gogh sunflowers above her desk.

"I hear that was some party at Emilio and Pilar's place!" she said with a mischievous grin.

I put my head in my hands.

"Relax, Laura," she said. "I don't think there's anybody clumsier than me! Last year, I knocked over the lemonade stand at the school's Spring Fling twice in the same afternoon." Her large frame shook with laughter, and I instantly felt much better. "Anyway," she concluded, echoing Bronwyn's remark of the previous evening, "that tent manufacturer ought to be sued!"

I would never be one of Metropolitan's alpha moms, I thought, but at least it didn't matter to Sunny.

"So . . . what did you think of the prospective parents we just met?" she asked playfully.

"They all seem very nice," I said neutrally. "It's interesting to see the process from the other side."

Sunny sighed, took off her glasses, and folded them on the desk. "I wish we had the facilities to accommodate more children at Metropolitan," she said, shaking her head with genuine regret. "Believe me, I've struggled with this issue, since there are so many stellar and deserving families out there. But we simply can't do it without either carving more classrooms out of the limited space we have or increasing class size."

She paused for a few moments and clasped her hands together thoughtfully in her signature gesture.

"For a while, you know, I even thought about purchasing a second building and creating an annex," she said. "Other downtown schools, like Little Red and Washington Market, have expanded their facilities, so I thought, *Why not Metropolitan?* But in the end, I decided against it. I think the intimacy we maintain at Metropolitan is so much more appropriate for children at this early and tender stage in their lives."

I had to agree with her. For the first time, I saw the situation from her point of view. She had struggled for years to provide quality preschool education to children of the neighborhood's garment-factory workers, and later its influx of artists and bohemians. But the city had evolved, property values had bubbled, and TriBeCa now had a population of wealthy new parents who viewed Metropolitan and the other private TriBeCa preschools as hot properties. If people like Sunny hadn't adapted to the new realities, they wouldn't be here anymore.

She pulled out a yellow notepad, wrote my name at the top, and said, "Now, I'm sorry, but I have to ask you a few questions regarding the unpleasant incident with the class pet the other day. Don't worry, it's just a formality. Shall we begin?"

I nodded.

"Good! Let's start with Anna's history. Is she on any medications?"

"No!"

"Good! Does she have any history of behavioral problems we should know about?"

"No!"

"Good! Any disturbances on the home front? Mommy and Daddy having any trouble getting along?"

"No!" I flinched inside. In my mind's eye I could still see Anna, eyes squeezed shut, hands pressed to her ears to drown out the sounds of our bickering.

"Excellent! Has Anna had any visits with mental-health professionals?"

"No!"

"Of course not!" Sunny said.

I felt another pang of guilt, this time for fibbing about Anna's appointment with a therapist. But Sunny didn't seem to notice.

"Well, that does it," she said, smiling with satisfaction.

"That's it?" I asked, feeling a bit dirty inside.

"Yes!"

"What about Snowflake?"

She looked slightly aggrieved.

"We all miss Snowflake," she intoned. She reached over and held my arm. "Listen, Laura, we are going to care of . . . the situation. I know and you know that you don't have to worry. The stages of children's development might seem alarming to the first-time parent, but they are absolutely nothing to worry about, especially if you're an old pro like me." She gave a hearty laugh, and the large opal on her bosom glistened in the sunlight.

"Besides," she added, "boys will be . . ."

She caught herself abruptly. "I mean, I will be speaking to all of the parents. But I would appreciate it if you would refrain from sharing the details of our conversation with the other mothers. You know how they get very nervous about this kind of thing."

I nodded, already mentally editing the conversation I knew I'd inevitably have about it with Bronwyn and Dominique.

Sunny's phone buzzed and she put it on speakerphone.

"Your next appointment is here," her secretary chirped.

The meeting was over. Sunny gave me a final smile as I walked to the open door. At that moment, Tori happened to be walking her class to the music room. Anna glanced toward the door with fatal precision and saw me.

"*Mommy!*" she yelled and lunged in my direction. Then she threw herself on the floor. Flailing her arms and legs, she screamed at the top of her lungs. "I'm a cat-cow *baby*! I want my mommy! Waah!"

I ran over to her and quietly ordered her to get up.

"I can't walk! Baby cat-cows need to be carried!" she wailed.

I reached down to pick her up, but she was so deep into her baby act that she accidentally hit me in the face with her little fist.

My cheek stung. I felt a hot flash of anger. Why did Anna have to throw her fit right here, right now? Didn't she realize how much damage she was doing to her own future? And to me? What was wrong with her? Was she a hamster murderer? For the first time, the horrible doubt crossed my mind. What if the parents of Metropolitan were right? What if I was a rotten parent, with an ailing marriage and a disturbed child who deserved professional attention instead of a scholarship?

"Get up!" I ordered again, louder this time. "*Now!*"

"Carry me!"

I grabbed my daughter by the shoulders in an attempt to at least keep her still. She looked up at me with a startled expression, then began crying for real in giant, heaving sobs.

I was instantly filled with remorse. *What is wrong with me?* I lifted her up and cradled her. She whimpered on my breast. I felt awful, more awful than I could remember. *Get a grip, Laura,* I told myself. I looked up and saw Tori shepherding her class away. Sunny was standing in her doorway, a look of surprise on her face. Beside her, I saw Sunny's next visitors.

Kim and Amy.

Kim eyed me, cool and knowing. Amy wore a falsely ingratiating smile.

"Hey, Laura, great to see you again," Amy said a bit too brightly, as though we'd just bumped into each other on an afternoon stroll. "Anna and Anna had such a great time playing together the other day. Did Richard tell you about the amazing coincidence? Wesley and I live in the same building as *your* Anna's therapist!"

Bitch! I gritted my teeth furiously. I glanced at Sunny and saw a strange look pass over her eyes. Flashing daggers at Amy, I clutched Anna tightly and headed for the door.

Chapter 8

I spy
With my little eye . . .

Dominique was wearing large tortoiseshell sunglasses and a wide-brimmed red fedora, wrapped in place with a gauzy veil tied around her ears and under her chin. She looked liked a Technicolor-era leading lady traveling incognito. I wasn't much more convincing. I was striving for the inconspicuous librarian look with a shapeless blazer over a tweed skirt, my hair pulled into a tight bun. Unfortunately, we were the only women in the Hotel Gansevoort's lobby who were not wearing skinny jeans and sparkly tops, and the third-tier models that served as the hotel staff kept shooting us snooty looks. We had positioned ourselves on the cushy divans by the large glass windows in front so that we could keep an eye on the street and the entrance to the hotel.

"How do you think Bronwyn is getting on?" I asked Dominique. At this very moment, Bronwyn was having her meeting with Sunny to discuss the hamster incident. "You guys will be okay without me, won't you?" Bronwyn had said anxiously as we parted at the drop-off.

"Oh, she will get what she wants," Dominique replied airily. "Bronwyn always knows what she wants. It is okay, if you do not want a lot. *I* want too much!"

Dominique quickly slipped back into her favorite subject. We were on chapter thirty-nine or so of the oral history of her life and loves.

Her father, she told me, had been a professional skier. But when he was twenty-seven and she was just five, he took a fatal plunge during a jumping competition. Her mother was a carefree beauty whose grief turned to depression. A subsequent marriage to a wealthy, much older man made everything worse. She did it, she told Dominique bitterly, "so that you and your sister can have a good life," and retreated into alcoholism. Dominique rebelled against the stultifying world of upper-crust Lyons.

So it was on to the bright lights of Paris, the stage, and the cinema.

And then she met Alan.

I learned that there was much more to Alan than the square-jawed shopping mall developer I had met at Pilar and Emilio's rooftop party. Alan's father had been a spy with the National Security Agency, and they had lived all over the world. Finally, when Alan entered junior high school, the family settled in Miami. Alan's father instructed young Alan to keep his position a secret. But one day at school, Alan said too much. Word got around town, and Alan's father was redeployed to Hong Kong, where his cover wouldn't be blown. His mother joined his father, leaving Alan behind in the care of his grandmother.

"Alan was like me in that way," Dominique said. "He was accustomed to thinking for himself. But unlike me, he always longed for a normal life."

Alan turned to the stability of schooling as a refuge from his loneliness. He earned good grades, entered a top university, and started his own real-estate development firm. But he had never trusted anyone enough to reveal the story of his past. Until he met Dominique.

When they first met, he spoke almost incessantly of his childhood. Within a few months, she discovered that she had become pregnant. Alan was thrilled. There was a hasty marriage. And suddenly, everything changed: directors broke their promises, her agent started avoiding her phone calls.

"And all the things I spent my life running away from turned out to be all of the things that make Alan happy," Dominique said flatly. "Stability. Predictability. They are the enemy of passion. Do you not agree with me?"

She must have caught the look on my face.

"I know what you are thinking, Laura. You think I am spoiled."

I smiled. *Busted!*

"Well——" I started to say, but Dominique cut me off.

"I have seen that look before. 'She has everything. A nice husband, a beautiful child, good health, plenty of money.' But just because people have these things does not mean that they are happy. Life is not an application form. No one gives you credit for checking off the boxes. Then you get these things you think you want. And so what? There should be more meaning to life. Otherwise, we are just like cows. Happy in the fields, chewing our grass. Not thinking. Not living. Waiting for the *chop!*" Her hand sliced through the air.

I knew that despite the overacting, Dominique was genuinely unhappy. Personally, right now, I wanted a whole lot less drama in my life. There were too many things going on at once. Too many issues, too many demands impossible to meet. Sometimes I felt like a juggler with both hands tied behind my back, just waiting for everything to land on top of me with a great big splat. But when I thought of how empty Bronwyn's marriage had seemed, I asked myself whether I wasn't just imagining more problems than I really had. Then I remembered that Richard had surreptitiously spent an evening with Amy. And I wondered if imagining dire consequences might just be a rational response to life.

"Maybe you need a purpose of some kind," I volunteered, trying to shake the thought. "Some kind of a job or—"

"Passion is what I need!" Dominique said fiercely, raising her head proudly as though facing down a battalion of enemy cattle rustlers. "I am not ambitious for my career anymore! I do not have a big American ego. I am a woman who is driven by emotion. By *passion*."

"Don't you and Alan have . . . *passion?*" I asked.

"I practically have to beg for it!" Dominique's voice went up an octave and her hands lifted with it. "Alan works late almost every night. When he comes home, he says he is tired. And when it happens, it's . . ." She made one of her Gallic expressions, sounding like *pfffft*. "You know."

Not really, I thought. Sex with Richard might not always be the multicourse epicurean feast that it had been when we first met. However, it was reliably good. Or at least it had been—before thoughts about Amy on a bearskin rug had begun to intrude and make me nauseated.

"Laura, what would you think if I said I had taken a lover? I mean really, what would you think in your heart?" Dominique's eyes bore into me and she thrust her finger into my chest.

"I'd think: Thank God *someone* has the energy to sleep around," I quipped. I was pretty sure that the question was hypothetical, but not totally sure. I thought of Amy again and I frowned.

"Oh, I would not sleep around." She opened her eyes wide. "I would not risk everything in my life for a stupid one-night stand. I want to hear a man, a *real* man, tell me again that he craves me, that he can't live without me, that I am the most beautiful woman in the world, that he cannot sleep or eat and thinks about me night and day. I need to feel that I am *alive*."

She stopped talking for a moment and inspected me.

"Laura, you look terrible," she pronounced flatly. She shook her head as though noticing my presence for the first time. "And your *hair*! It is a *disgrace*!" She gestured at my messy bun. "You are working too hard."

I sighed. "No, it's not work." Dominique had told me so much about her troubles that I decided to confide in her about mine. I filled her in on my most recent fight with Richard.

Dominique listened to my tale of domestic angst with serious eyes. "Love is so complicated," she said. "If only we could be like machines, or love only what is good for us. But the heart is unpredictable."

"What does love have to do with any of this?" I asked her, fuming. "You don't think Richard is in love with Amy?"

"No, he is in love with *you*," Dominique said bluntly. "But he is *intrigued* by Amy. Perhaps he wants to . . . how do you say . . . *experiment* something?"

A fresh wave of anger swept over me, mixed with fear.

"How can you tell?" I asked.

"It is obvious," she said. "He is a man, and men like to be flattered. More so than women, you know. A man can say to a beautiful woman, 'You are so beautiful,' and she will say, 'Really? But don't you think my hips are a bit big?' But you can tell a man who is frankly very ugly, 'You are a sex god,' and he will believe every word."

Both my anger and my fear increased. Even Dominique could see that Amy was trying to steal my husband! And Richard was letting her try! Amy was attacking me—and my daughter! I began to dream up punishments that I thought would suit the crime—gruesome, bone-crushing tortures.

"Amy is flattering him," Dominique concluded firmly. "And you are making it worse."

"*Me?*" I started to ask. "But how . . ."

Suddenly, Dominique straightened up in her chair and looked over my shoulder. "Oh my God! She does not even know how to dress for an affair!"

Kim was marching in a straight line toward the three side-by-side elevators in a prim, dark business suit. Her short hair fell flat against her head, and her lips were a hastily applied streak of red.

Just before she got to the elevator, a man came in from the

other side of the lobby and greeted her. He wore a large, round, pinstriped suit and had bad skin. I recognized him instantly.

"It's Wesley, Amy's husband," I hissed.

"*Mon Dieu!*" Dominique said. "No wonder Amy is flirting with your husband. *Her* husband is so ugly! And so kinky! It is going to be a *ménage à trois!*"

Then another man, younger and in a dark business suit, joined them at the elevator bank. The man had a computer and some sort of camera equipment slung over his shoulder.

We watched the lights on the elevator panel progress to the number four and stop. Then we quickly dashed for the next elevator, reaching the fourth floor just in time to see Kim and her kinky companions turning a corner at the end of a long corridor. We raced to follow, again catching sight of them just as they turned, this time into one of the rooms.

We had promised Bronwyn total surveillance. We paused for a moment and then, stiffening our resolve, walked gingerly down the hallway. Astonishingly, the door to the room was slightly ajar. With bated breath, we peeked inside.

Jeffrey was seated next to a projector on a large, oval table. His tie was slightly loosened around his collar. He had that same amused look I'd seen on him before, at Emilio and Pilar's party. It was as though he thought that life was one funny joke, and that we were all in it together. Without any effort, he seemed to set the tone of the room.

At his side, his young assistant tracked his every move. On the opposite side of the table sat Wesley, stiff and earnest. Compared to Jeffrey's klieg lights, he had all the glamour of a sputtering candle. Kim took a seat at the far end of the table, next to Wesley, her smile fixed on Jeffrey, too.

"You don't think maybe they will make love afterward?" Dominique whispered, sounding disappointed.

I shook my head. We had obviously stumbled in on a business meeting.

While Jeffrey plied Kim and Wesley with small talk, the young man fiddled with his laptop. Soon the projector next to Jeffrey began beaming images on a screen on the far wall.

"This is our promotional film," Jeffrey explained in his posh version of an Australian accent. "It's still in development, but we think you will find it entertaining."

Dominique and I repositioned ourselves in the hallway to get a better look, which also put us out of our quarry's sightlines.

New Agey pipe sounds began to issue from a pair of hidden speakers, and the screen filled with gorgeous tropical island scenes fading into one another: a white sandbar with three palm trees floating on a transparent, turquoise sea; the sun setting over the ocean, with the silhouette of a yacht on the horizon; pelicans soaring above limestone cliffs; a gleaming swimming pool surrounded by teak lawn chairs; a smiling Caribbean youth holding up a bowl of tropical fruit.

"Welcome to Iguana Cay," intoned a buttery female voice in the Queen's English. "Where life is sweeter than your sweetest dreams."

Dominique and I stared at the cascade of idyllic images. A hotel maid came by with her trolley, gave us an odd look, then peeked inside. She watched the show appreciatively for a few moments.

"A ten-minute boat ride from the international airport of

Providenciales, Iguana Cay is a world the way it was meant to be, your own private utopia—three square miles of tropical paradise. Nestled at the center of the island is the Main House of the Iguana Club, boasting a state-of-the-art spa staffed with internationally renowned yoga instructors and healing artists, a golf course and sports center, and a clubhouse with world-class dining. The island community numbers one hundred private Deluxe Bungalows with beach access; fifty Royal Villas, each with private swimming pool; and ten Imperial Estates, each with seven hundred fifty feet of ocean frontage, plus guest house, staff quarters, private gardens, and dock."

Images of handcrafted gazebos, massage tables, steamy whirlpool tubs, coral reefs bursting with sea life, grilled lobster on fine china plates, more beaches, and elegant, white-clay island-style homes wreathed in bougainvillea flitted across the screen. I pictured myself on horseback, galloping along the white sand, my hair blowing in the fresh sea breeze. In my vision I sensed a rider pulling up next to me on a powerful dappled charger. I glanced over, but it wasn't Richard. No, Richard was clinging to a life raft in the middle of the ocean, fending off the sharks that had just devoured the despicable Amy. Rather, on the dappled stallion was a different rider—Jeffrey.

"Construction is now almost complete," Jeffrey was saying, interrupting the video. A lock of brown hair had fallen across his eyes. I found myself mentally undressing him. Was his chest hairy or smooth? Boxers or briefs?

"Half a billion dollars in the making," the sultry voice of the video narrator continued, "Iguana Cay is more than a piece of incomparable real estate. It is a private club. Membership is a privilege. Each candidate must obtain the recommendations of three current club members in order to be considered. For those fortunate enough to obtain clearance from the board, memberships will be made available for private sale this spring, for occupancy beginning in the summer months."

Jeffrey clicked off the projector. "Well, I hope you found that amusing," he said, his eyes twinkling. "Bruce can fill you in on some of the numbers."

The younger man cleared his throat, shuffled some papers, and began to mumble in an unintelligible way about equity investments and tax efficiencies. I tried to follow what he was saying, reminding myself that the details might be important. But my mind quickly went into high-school-chemistry-class mode—none of the details stuck. Instead, I watched Jeffrey and Kim, trying to discern sparks of electricity between them. Nothing. Not enough to power a penlight.

"Can you tell us about pricing?" Kim interjected, somewhat impatiently.

"Naturally," Jeffrey said. He turned to the young man at his side. "Bruce, you have the figures," he said.

Bruce shuffled some more papers in front of him. "Provisionally, we are putting forward some sight-unseen prices, which are at a very substantial discount to what we expect the full price to be," he said. "The early-riser prices for rights to the Deluxe Bungalows are to begin at two hundred thousand dollars. The Royal Villas will start at three hundred thousand dollars. And the Imperial Estates are eight hundred thousand dollars and up."

"This sounds promising," Kim said briskly. "If we can offer these memberships on a cost-plus basis, with any premium coming to us as a charitable contribution, this could be a win-win for you . . . and for Metropolitan."

Wesley nodded in agreement.

Dominique and I exchanged glances of surprise and confusion.

"Cost-plus?" Jeffrey replied, hoisting an eyebrow. "Oh, my dear, you're going to ruin me."

"Hey, come on," Kim persisted. "It's great distribution for you. Plus, there are tax advantages. We'll get other schools involved, build up interest in the properties. It's a win-win."

Slowly, I was beginning to figure out the business deal we were witnessing. Jeffrey's company had one hundred sixty parcels of luxury Caribbean real estate to sell. Kim was proposing to help him by selling the properties through the Metropolitan auction. Jeffrey would accept a low, discounted rate on any properties sold, and Metropolitan would keep some kind of small commission, based on whatever surplus it could generate from the buyers in its parent body.

For a moment, I wondered if Kim's proposal was strictly legal. Then I realized: Of course it was. Metropolitan was a private institution, and Jeffrey was a private businessman. That gave them the right to do business that profited both, even if it was a somewhat untraditional way of raising money for a school.

The images of paradise in the Caribbean had given me a warm feeling, but suddenly the glow vanished. I realized that I would have been happier if we had in fact discovered Jeffrey and Kim licking yellowtail carpaccio off each other's bodies on a hotel mattress. Instead, she was using her power in a much more subtle way. She was going to make herself indispensable to the school as a top fundraiser, she was going to win favor with Jeffrey, and she was going to get a spot at Holyfield for her son without breaking any of the rules.

That was the difference between Kim and me. Kim was a player in New York; I was just a bystander. Her son could maim and kill a whole herd of hamsters, I realized, and my Anna would still end up doing time for the deed.

Wesley and Amy, too, for that matter, would find an easy welcome. Wesley seemed as dull as one of Anna's plastic play knives. But he could still buy his way into the club by throwing his firm's money around.

"You do drive a hard bargain," Jeffrey said at last. "Alright, then," he continued, exhaling. "You win. I mean, we win. I mean, we win-win. Bruce will write it up."

"Great," Kim said. "Oh, that's my office," she added, glancing at her BlackBerry as it buzzed. "Excuse me, please. I have to take this call outside."

Before I had time to think, Kim was heading straight for the door. Dominique and I exchanged panicked glances. It was time to disappear. I sprinted back toward the elevator. I looked behind me and saw Dominique moving the other way, but her high heel caught on the carpet and she stumbled. Her getaway aborted, she ducked behind a pillar just as Kim appeared in the doorway, her hand clutching her BlackBerry to her ear. As far as I could tell, she had seen nothing.

I loitered briefly in the lobby, hoping Dominique would find her way down, but I didn't see her. She was probably waiting for a good moment to escape. Was there a back exit on the other side of the building? I glanced at my watch. It was past noon. I would have to hustle if I was going to pick up Anna from school on time. I decided to go.

I walked a few blocks to the subway at Fourteenth Street and Seventh Avenue and descended into the crowded station. I ran my Metrocard through the turnstile and hopped on the number 1 train downtown. The subway car was full, and I politely trained my eyes above my fellow passengers' heads, to the beer commercials. In my mind, I mentally reconstructed the pitch meeting where the advertising agency pushed the strategy on their client. "Think 'urban sex,' " the agency team leader was saying. "Young, hip, multicultural. You know, throw in a couple of body piercings and tattoos. They're hot, they're hooking up, and they're using your beer to do it."

"Urban sex" wasn't my world anymore. But then again, the exclusive, ultrapampered world of Bloom ladies, with their $500 haircuts and $1,000 handbags, wasn't my world, either. I began to wonder if I still belonged in the city.

I closed my eyes and tried to picture myself in Iguana Cay. I saw Kim, Bronwyn, and Dominique in brightly colored frocks, hosting a lavish sunset party in an imperial estate, the jasmine-scented air full of laughter and gentle island music. Richard, in his brown suit and hiking boots, was there, linked arm-in-arm with Amy, who was wearing her sleeveless cocktail sheath, a hibiscus flower tucked fetchingly behind her ear. Anna and I were watching it all from a distance—the sole residents in an undeveloped part of the island, our trailer sandwiched on a scrubby patch of dirt between a power station and a waste-treatment plant.

Chapter 9

To market, to market, to buy a fat pig
Home again, home again, jiggety-jig

Dominique held a shimmering dress up to her neck and frowned into the mirror. The scrawny sales assistant hovered around her like a hummingbird, prodding and poking the dress to move it around her hips. "It's a bit glitter-rock, but still dressed up," she said. "Like, maybe with crimped hair?"

"It makes me look fat," Dominique announced, returning the dress without a glance. "I need something a bit more . . ." She made vague gestures with her hands.

The salesgirl seemed to understand the assignment and scurried off.

Dominique had cornered me that morning at drop-off.

"Laura, you must come with me!" she insisted. "I can't bear to face Madison Avenue alone!" It turned out that she was no longer happy with the things "Isaac" was sending her. "He thinks I am a grande dame now—an old lady!" She huffed. "I need to do *everything* myself!"

Eager to review our discoveries at the Gansevoort the day before, I acquiesced. After dropping off our girls in Tori's classroom, Dominique led me outside to a dark blue town car purring at the curb. I reached for the chrome door handle, but within seconds Alan was standing beside me.

"I'm playing driver this morning," he said playfully. In his well-cut navy suit, he looked tall and fit. He had a roguish grin on his face, and his eyes twinkled. For the first time, I noticed they were bright blue. Amused, I did a small curtsy.

Alan raced to the other side of the car to get Dominique's door. I watched his eyes follow her intently from behind, and he put his hand tenderly on her shoulder.

Dominique, evidently irritated by her husband's driver act, flounced into the tan leather interior next to me. "Where to, ma'am?" Alan chirped from the driver's seat.

"*Mais Alain, c'est absurde!* Take us to Dolce & Gabbana," Dominique ordered, somewhat irritably. The car jolted gently into action, and we pulled away from Metropolitan and into traffic.

"I think they are the only ones making interesting dresses this season," she said to me as an aside.

As we headed uptown, Dominique stared out the window while Alan and I competed for who had the worst New York City taxi driver story to tell. I could tell from the way he talked that he would rather have been motoring on the leafy streets of some tranquil suburb, and I knew from the way he had looked at Dominique that she was very much a part of his dream. When we arrived, Alan cheerfully opened my door, still relishing his chauffeur act. It crossed my mind that he must be an excellent parent. But before he could get to Dominique, she was already on the sidewalk.

Alan turned to me.

"So, how's Richard doing with that academic paper he mentioned at the party?" he asked, clearly stalling for time with Dominique.

"Oh, it's going well," I replied with an ingratiating smile. Dominique's casual attitude toward her husband seemed so inexplicable. I felt embarrassed on his behalf.

"Well, good to see you again," he said awkwardly. "I'd better get back to the office." We shook hands and I turned to join Dominique, who was already through the heavy glass doors of the boutique.

Now, ensconced in the elegant shop, with its wares displayed like museum pieces, I was ready to hear Dominique's take on the events at the Gansevoort.

But Dominique seemed absorbed in her shopping mission, throwing one fringed shawl after another over her neck. I pulled a cropped brocade jacket off the rack and tried it on for size. A glance at the price tag confirmed that it easily cost more than Richard's after-tax salary for a month. I wondered what life would be like if my credit cards had no limits.

"So?" I persisted. "Doesn't it seem a little over-the-top that Kim has organized this big development deal with Jeffrey and Wesley?"

"It is a . . . small outrage," Dominique replied. "But it is not a big one. And it will not work."

"Why not?" I demanded. But her eye had caught on a floor-length gown across the room. She took hold of me and we swept over. The sales assistant came rushing up behind us with an armload of clothes. "In a moment, *cherie!*" Dominique said, waving her off in a slightly peeved tone. "Of course!" the assistant replied, retreating to a respectful distance.

"In fact, I have some interesting news about Kim," Dominique said. "She is truly desperate."

"Desperate! Really? Why?"

"You must wait until Bronwyn gets here first."

Dominique ducked into the dressing room. A few moments later, she pushed aside the curtain dramatically. She twirled in front of the mirror. The long, shimmery, sea-green gown hugged her neat curves like algae on a mermaid. "This is it!" she exclaimed with satisfaction. The salesgirl nodded. Assessing her reflection in the mirror, Dominique was having a private moment with herself. She posed with one hip cocked, like a 1960s silver-screen sex kitten, lowering her gaze into an insouciant expression. For a moment, I caught a glimpse of the elegant movie star she once was. I wondered where she was planning to wear it.

"Hi, girls!" I heard Bronwyn say behind us.

Her pale hair was pulled off her face into a high ponytail. But today her smile seemed tight. She was like a rubber band twisted white around a pencil.

"What are we going to do about Kim?" I turned to her.

Her smile shifted ever so slightly, turning into a grimace. "Oh my God. You would not *believe* what that woman is doing," Bronwyn said. "It isn't enough for her to try to buy Eve and Jeffrey with that Iguana Cay project. She's still got to cover up for her kid. I checked with Dan, my psychologist friend. You know what he thinks Jake has?"

She paused for dramatic effect.

"APD," she said.

"No way!"

"Yes way!"

I paused. "So what *is* APD?"

"Antisocial Personality Disorder. It's basically a fancy name for sociopaths. Criminologists call it 'the lifer category.' There's no hope of recovery. That's Jake to a T. He doesn't empathize with animals, so he thinks it's okay to kill them! But wait, it gets worse. If he starts to put people in the same category, watch out!" She drew an imaginary knife across her throat. "You know, Jeffrey Dahmer killed animals when he was a kid. . . ."

I looked at Bronwyn in horror. She absentmindedly accepted a mohair sweater handed to her by *cherie* and tried it on. "That looks great," the saleswoman said, but Bronwyn continued talking like a machine with no off button.

"Get this. I caught her *lying*! She told Sunny she was taking Jake to the zoo after school. So Bernadette watched her after her nanny dropped the kid off at the Starbucks on Twenty-seventh and First. They went straight to Bellevue, just like we thought!"

Dominique returned from the dressing room glowing with contentment. Having overheard the last snatches of our conversation, she said, "Oh, but there is something I must tell you! You girls are going to love this!"

"What?" Bronwyn and I said in unison.

"Kim is doing more than just organizing this Iguana Cay sale with Jeffrey," Dominique whispered. "She's buying a house there in advance for herself, before anybody else has a chance to place a bid!"

"That's . . . that's not fair!" Bronwyn exclaimed.

"It is true," Dominique continued. "She is making the deal already, just to be sure that she gets the house she wants! A bungalow deluxe or whatever it is! One of the small ones! A pied-à-terre in the Caribbean. But the reason she chose this one is it is closest to Jeffrey's house, it is practically on his property, it is the only house he can see from his terrace. So they will be neighbors!"

I was starting to piece together Kim's plot. She was going to make herself the school's chief financial officer, raising hundreds of thousands of dollars, maybe even get a new school building named after herself. And she was going to get in good with Jeffrey and Eve. She would vacation with them, let them play with her kid on the beach, and eventually secure a coveted letter of recommendation. Bronwyn was right: She would stop at nothing to get Jake into Holyfield.

"She's cheating!" Bronwyn fumed. "She won't get away with this!"

"How do you know this?" I asked Dominique. At the meeting in the hotel, I remembered, I hadn't heard Kim say anything about buying one of the of the Iguana Cay memberships for herself.

"I learned some very interesting things after you left," Dominique said with a wink. "It is too bad you had to rush away!"

"What are we going to do?" I wailed. "Kim is going to frame Anna for Snowflake's murder!"

Bronwyn looked at me with alarm. She seemed almost paralyzed with outrage.

"Oh my God, you're right! She's going to make it impossible for them to get rid of Jake, and then she's going to let one of our kids take the blame!"

She seemed to ruminate for a few moments, her eyes darting anxiously back and forth. "I'm calling Lloyd," she finally announced to no one in particular.

She picked up her cell phone and speed-dialed her husband. It took her a few minutes to get past his assistants, but she finally succeeded in tracking him down.

"Hi, honey," I heard her say in a falsely casual tone. As she drifted off to the other side of the room, I heard her tell the story in snatches. "Who cares how I know? . . . If Kim does this, she's going to sneak her son into Holyfield, and we're going to lose our chance with both of our kids! . . . We have to stop her. . . . I *am* calm. . . . I *am* keeping my voice down. . . . Listen, Lloyd, you owe me this . . . as a courtesy . . ."

When Bronwyn returned, I was sitting glumly on a lounge chair, watching Dominique try on another frock, this one with elaborate ruching around the bust. I looked at Bronwyn with somber eyes.

"Relax, Laura," Bronwyn said. She put her arm around me. "I think we're going to get this problem under control."

"How?" I asked.

"Lloyd will take care of it," she said calmly. "We're going to buy a Royal Villa."

Chapter 10

Horsie, horsie, don't you stop
Just let your feet go clippety-clop

From the moment I had left Bronwyn and Dominique at the Madison Avenue boutique with a smile on my face and the absolute conviction that I was completely and utterly on my own, I had known the time had come for drastic measures.

The others would have no trouble protecting their children. All Bronwyn had to do was toss $300,000 at the problem. She could just take it out of her furniture budget for a couple years. And she'd get a Royal Villa in which to vacation alongside the people who pulled the strings at all the best private schools in Manhattan.

All Dominique had to do was put on a pretty dress and remind everyone that she was a film star.

All Kim had to do was lie, cheat, and make deals. Harrison, Jake, and Emmy would all end up at Holyfield, where they would become buddies, take drugs together, and then get accepted to Princeton. Meanwhile, Anna would be serving a sentence for second-degree hamster murder in the local penitentiary, otherwise known as our neighborhood public school.

I realized that I had long since passed the point where I could calm myself with the mantra "It's just preschool." For better or for worse, it was now my life.

So I had been forced to take matters into my own hands. It was one of those crisp autumn days when the skies are clear and the sun seems strangely cold. I lurked outside Metropolitan, wearing a baseball hat and sunglasses, in a taxicab with the meter running. Anna was safely tucked away in an after-school class for the next three hours. *Or maybe not so safely,* I thought with a shudder. Today was Classical Music Day. Sunny insisted Baroque compositions were optimal for developing children's spatial reasoning skills. But Anna hated Bach with a passion.

I watched the meter click its way up into the double digits and silently fumed at Kim's nanny, Betty, for being so slow. Finally, I saw Betty step out the front door with Jake. I hunched down in my seat. As usual, Jake was in a stroller, his long limbs spilling out over the sturdy frame. *Four years old and still strolling,* I thought. *Definitely a psycho.*

Betty parked the stroller on the sidewalk, then stepped out into the street and lifted up her hand to hail a cab. Several of them passed her before one finally stopped. I had often seen cabbies get out from behind the wheel to help white mothers load up their tots and strollers. But I'd never seen one help a nanny. Several more clicks went by as Jake climbed into the backseat and Betty folded the cumbersome stroller and stuffed it into the trunk. As she finally levered herself in next to the boy, I said the words that every New Yorker secretly longs to say at least once: "Follow that cab!"

We trailed our quarry up West Broadway through SoHo and turned right on Houston Street. We passed the Mercury Lounge, where I'd squandered my youth chasing skinny guys in promo T-shirts for obscure indie bands. But there was no time to reminisce, and we turned left on First Avenue. On Twenty-fourth Street we got snarled up at a traffic light. In a panic, I threw a wad of bills at my cabbie and jumped out. I ran the three blocks up to the Starbucks at Twenty-seventh Street.

As I approached, huffing from the effort, I saw Betty loading Jake back into the stroller. The look of weary resignation on her face hadn't changed. I slowed to a brisk walk, trying to make myself inconspicuous. Sure enough, Kim emerged, steaming latte in hand. She spoke briefly with her nanny, then began pushing her boy across the street toward the large medical center. By the time I reached the hospital, Kim was already through the front door.

I paused for a moment, wondering if I had truly lost my mind. Here I was, chasing another mother into a hospital. Was this really necessary? Under ordinary circumstances, I would be way out of line. But now I could almost hear Bronwyn's warnings resonating in my ears. I reminded myself that my daughter's future was at stake—and perhaps even her safety. The mental image of Snowflake's inert body spurred me forward.

I pulled out my camera phone and pretended to make a call while I snapped away. If I was going to take on someone as powerful as Kim, I figured I was going to need hard evidence. I shuffled impatiently through the oversized mechanical revolving door and then stumbled hurriedly into the lobby. I was so disconcerted and out of breath by this time that I somehow jammed the cell phone camera, and began pushing buttons in a panic.

I didn't see the white-haired lady in the wheelchair.

My pants caught on a lever protruding from her vehicle, and I flew sprawling onto the floor.

"Hey! Watch where ya goin'!" the white-haired lady shouted in a surprisingly loud voice. All around me in the lobby, people stopped and turned to look at the commotion.

I pulled myself onto my knees and looked up. Kim was staring down at me.

"*You!*" she spat. "Haven't you had enough of assaulting me! If you come near me again, I'm going to call the police!"

"I'm not assaulting you!" I said, suddenly flustered, as I stood up and brushed myself off. "I'm just a klutz, okay?"

"What are you doing here?" she demanded. *She* was mad at *me*? This was too much.

"I thought I would ask you the same question," I shot back.

She suddenly looked frightened.

"No, you don't have to tell me," I continued, gathering my courage. "I already know!" I glanced at my phone. Miraculously, it was in camera mode again and ready to take photos. I held it out and pointed it at her and Jake, and it lit them up with a flash. "I think Sunny will enjoy seeing pictures of you and Jake going to the . . . *zoo!*" I blurted.

"How dare you take pictures of us!" Kim reached for her son protectively.

"Why not?" I took another. "Hey, I'm being investigated be-cause your pal Amy told Sunny I took my daughter to a therapist *just once*! I think Sunny has a right to know if one of her students is getting treatment *twice a week* at a *psych ward*."

"Wait!" she said, sounding panicked. "It's not what you think!"

"I bet it *is* what I think!" I roared with indignation. "And if you think you can go around suggesting there's something wrong with Anna, then I have a right to let everyone know where Jake spends his afternoons!"

"I don't know what are you talking about! And I don't think you do, either!"

I caught a puzzled look on Jake's face. He tugged at Kim from his seat in the stroller. "Mommy, can we go in now?"

"Yes, my darling," she said. Kim seemed to compose herself. The tenderness in her voice surprised me. I looked closely at her eyes, and for the first time I noticed how delicate and beautiful they were. She had fine little wrinkles, like crepe paper, radiating from their corners. I had been carrying around an image of her in my head, the hard-edged face of a bitter, cynical, and ruthless woman, but now I thought I was looking at someone else alto-gether. How well did I really know her?

"Mommy!"

She stroked her son's head and looked at me.

"I have to go, Laura," she said sadly.

"I . . ." I faltered. Then I clutched my cell phone and waved it vaguely in front of her. "I'm going to have to report . . ."

"You *can't*!"

"I *will*!"

She looked very uncertain. A small bead of moisture glistened off her eyes. I thought I saw a pleading look on her face. Finally, as though surrendering, she seemed to make up her mind.

"Follow me, then," she said quietly. "But please . . ." Her voice drifted off.

We rode the elevator in silence. Jake looked at me with curiosity. When he saw me looking back, he hid his flushed face behind his mother's leg, then peeped out again quizzically. Screwing up his courage, he flashed me a winning smile.

"My mommy bought me some LEGOs," he announced excitedly as the elevator car rose to the fourth floor. "I'm going to make a train!" Again, he smiled a proud, adorable smile. Rather than the deranged hamster killer I'd been picturing, he seemed like a nice, normal kid on a routine outing with his mother. Could there have been some mistake?

We passed a receptionist who waved at Kim. "Hi, Jake!" the lady said as we walked down a hallway.

Kim took Jake out of his stroller and picked him up. She hugged him with fierce affection. She glanced at me, her eyes wet. Then we entered a private room.

There was a bed and a television on at low volume. On the bed was a man who wore slippers and a blue hospital johnny. He had reddish hair and a four-day-old beard, and he looked thin and frail. He trembled a little when he saw us come in. His eyes and face had a kind of hollowed-out, prematurely aged look that I knew all too well. I had seen it on my own brother, James.

The familiar pain came back. I remembered those days I had tried so hard to forget. The long, agonizing fits; the sordid hunt for evidence of relapse; the endless, empty afternoons of watching, waiting, hoping for nothing to happen; the sheer inanity of the recovery rituals; and the haunting realization that the person who was destined to emerge from the rehabilitation process would be so much less bright a light than the irrepressible little boy I'd played with every day when we were young.

The man lifted a shaky hand. In an instant, I knew who he was and what we were doing here.

"Jake!" he said, his voice wavering.

"Daddy!" Jake said, bounding up on the bed.

Chapter 11

Here am I, Little Jumping Joan
When nobody's with me, I'm all alone

"They were true believers," Kim said with a wry smile. "They adopted me because they wanted to save my soul." I glanced outside the large side window of Bubby's restaurant and watched the people passing by on the sidewalk.

After we left the hospital, Jake's nanny had picked him up and taken him to a tumbling class. Kim and I had headed here, to Bubby's, a heavily themed "down-home American" restaurant on Hudson Street. The sloppy joes and apple pie were adequate at best—but the waiters were patient to the point of saintly with the neighborhood kids, bringing them free balloons and offering coloring books and crayons.

Feeling very penitent, I had begged Kim to join me for a bite. I needed to hear her side of the story.

"I guess work can wait," she had said grudgingly.

While Kim spoke, I nibbled on my soggy Caesar salad and tried to imagine what it must have been like to grow up as the only person of Korean descent in small-town Utah. I sensed that Kim was eyeing me carefully. She was incredibly slow to trust, I knew. I had forced myself into her life, and now she had shared with me more than she'd probably told anyone else at Metropolitan. I felt I had been given an extraordinary, fragile gift, and I desperately wanted her to know that I would guard it with all my power.

She was born in Korea and had no memory of her biological father. He was conscripted during the war, then disappeared. She and her birth mother scraped out a living on the outskirts of Seoul. Her mother supported them by selling soap, used cooking oil, anything she could get her hands on. "I remember a man offering her money to have sex with him," Kim said. "She refused. But that's how a lot of women survived at the time. Men would visit, and their kids would have to hide in the closet." She shivered. "My mother always said she dreamed of a better life for me."

When Kim was nine, her mother finally got a real beau, a businessman from downtown Seoul. He took them to a restaurant and bought Kim and her mother some new clothes. But Kim didn't trust him. One night at dinner, he snapped at Kim for serving herself first. "You are not my father!" she yelled. "I don't have to listen to you." Finally, he proposed to Kim's mother. But there was a catch. He would marry her—provided she send her daughter to live somewhere else.

"I remember my mother weeping all the way to the airport," Kim said. "She promised over and over again she'd come and get me back soon." She paused, swallowing hard. "Then . . . *he* grabbed me out of her arms and dragged me to the plane. He'd bought me a one-way ticket to America. That was the last time I saw her. Four months later, she had a disastrous miscarriage. She hemorrhaged to death."

Kim's adoptive parents had three older kids who were unfailingly nice to her. But she had arrived determined not to make the mistake of getting attached to anyone ever again. Anyway, they were already teenagers, and they were deeply involved with missionary work.

"Chuck and Diane are very decent people," Kim said, "but they didn't know what to do with me. I mean, their lives revolve around the church. They meant well. But I was from another solar system."

Kim shied away from the pieties of church life and devoted herself to school. Her adoptive family watched from a distance as she got accepted to the Massachusetts Institute of Technology and landed her first job as a professional in New York. They visited once, briefly, until Diane got a migraine and they boarded the plane back to Utah. Though Kim was still in touch with her adoptive parents, her trips home became less frequent.

"They've seen Jake only twice," she said. "They mainly want to know if we're taking him to church. They never warmed to Eric. Of course, they have no idea what's really happening to him now. I don't have the heart to tell them the truth. They think he has Lyme disease."

"I'm sorry I chased you into the hospital," I volunteered.

"Hey, it's okay, Laura," she said with a sad smile. "You know, I thought you were one of them."

I shook my head. I didn't know whose side I was on anymore.

"You wouldn't believe the hospital bills. . . ."

"Don't you have health insurance?" I asked.

"Yes, but it only covers so much," she said. "Eric's been in treatment on and off for almost two years now."

She stopped, choking briefly on her words.

I put my hand on her arm.

"He had so much drive," she said. "When he started his company, at the height of the dot-com boom, competition was so intense. Clients needed stuff turned around so fast. Eric had a couple dozen people working for him, but it was never enough. He stayed at the office until midnight every night. Then the bubble burst. Eric had to fire eighty percent of his staff. The pressure really got to him. He started snorting coke to stay awake and make his deadlines."

"Jake was a baby then," she continued in a tone of weary resignation, "and Eric kept talking about how much it costs to have a family in New York. It was like he aged ten years in six months. He became totally paranoid and started to smell like chemicals. But I honestly had no idea what was going on. One day he came home with a nasty burn on his arm. We went to the hospital, and the doctor took me aside. They told me he had been freebasing crystal meth."

I cringed. I had seen the kind of devastation drug addiction wreaked on a user's body, his mind, life.

"Eric really wants to be a good daddy. And I grew up without a father, so I know how important it is to have one. I can't let what happened to me happen to Jake. Eric loves Jake—I know he does! He loves him more than anything. Anything except . . ." she trailed off.

"I know," I broke in. "I know a little bit about these things. My brother, James . . ."

I faltered. I clung tightly to my images of Jamie as the sixth-grade whiz-kid, the prankster who left mystery limericks around the house to tease the family. When those images faded like old snapshots, I focused intently on how he was now, tanned and sober, teaching schoolchildren on an Indian reservation in Colorado. Seeing Eric had reminded me of the other James, the James from those long, chaotic years in between.

"James had a drug problem, too," I said to Kim. "Heroin mostly. He's clean now," I added brightly, wishing to convey some hope. It was true. For the first time in many years, James seemed happy. I was proud of how he'd pulled his life back together. But he wasn't quite the Jamie of his youth, full of childhood promise. The markers for success had been totally revised. For a guy like him, just having a girlfriend was like winning the Super Bowl.

Kim looked at me with a flash of surprise, which quickly turned to understanding.

"He's better now?" she said hopefully.

I smiled uncertainly. She shook her head, and I knew I didn't have to tell her anything more.

She folded her napkin and put it to the side, as though she were carefully encasing all of our feelings and storing them for safety.

"I can't let the school know," she announced flatly. "They think Eric is one of those management consultants who is always on the road. If they find out he's in long-term, inpatient rehab . . ."

I knew.

"They won't say anything. They'll just file me and Jake in the 'problem' category. Have you noticed how every parent in the school seems happily married?"

She was right. Even couples who were probably speaking to each other only through their lawyers put on a happy face before coming to school.

"I won't tell anyone," I promised.

"You know what it's like at Metropolitan. Lately I've started feeling like I'm back in junior high all over again!"

I laughed. I had to agree.

"I mean, these women remind me of these awful girls I knew in high school. They would say things like, 'Oh, you're Oriental, so of course you're good in math.' I spent ninth grade eating at a table all by myself in the cafeteria because the popular girls told everyone to stay away."

So she'd been excluded by the "in" crowd, too. I knew that dynamic all too well. I told her the story about Erin and Jennie from my old school days. Erin and Jennie were the "it" girls in my ninth-grade class. One day they started talking to me, pretending to be best friends after having previously treated me with all the dignity of a gym bag. They told me that Candies were really in, and said how much they each wanted to buy a pair. So when I got home I pestered my mom to buy them for me, which was a big deal because she thought they were trashy. The next day I showed up wearing my Candies. Jennie and Erin laughed uproariously. "Laura's wearing hooker shoes," they told everybody. "She thinks she's so hot!" They'd planned it all as a joke.

"And I thought you were one of them," Kim said, laughing softly to herself. "I mean, when you jumped on me at that party . . ."

"It was an accident! I swear!"

Kim looked at me and smiled. "Yeah, I guess I overreacted." I realized that Kim had a certain tone deafness when it came to understanding the Metropolitan social scene. She had seen me with Bronwyn and Dominique, and so she had assumed that I belonged to the same kind of society that they did. But I felt just as much like a fish out of water as she.

Then I had another thought.

"But what about the Iguana Cay project?" I asked. "I thought that was your way of trying to get favor with the school. . . ."

"Oh, it's a typical cosponsor deal," Kim said. "It's very common these days for land-development deals to have a charitable component. Usually to satisfy environmental or community concerns. In the case of Iguana Cay, the charitable component is the school." She faltered. "You and Bronwyn seemed like such expert party planners, I figured it was the least I could do. To tell the truth, I haven't got the time for this. It's crunch time at my job, and I barely get to see my son as it is. I've been taking a lot of the Iguana Cay project on faith and putting off the due diligence. Ordinarily, I'd spend weeks researching all the details before brokering the deal."

I looked at Kim again, her dark eyes fiercely intelligent, and I realized how remarkable she was. She had taken more outrageous blows in her life than most people do in their nightmares, and yet she had survived. In fact, she had triumphed. She had made a great career for herself, and she was raising a fine boy on her own. It made me feel good about New York City all over again. All the extremes were here in one place, from the extremely insane to the extremely talented. It made sense that someone like Kim, with one life story in Korea and another in Utah, would end up feeling at home in Manhattan.

"That Bronwyn—she's a piece of work!" Kim suddenly exclaimed.

I avoided her look. Bronwyn had been so wrong about Kim. But she had been so helpful to me. She had made me a part of the school; she had rescued me from social disaster at Serena's birthday party; she had even stood by me after the tent fell down around us. I knew that some of her affection was motivated by a desire to appear philanthropic—I was, after all, the mother of Metropolitan's Forsythe Scholarship recipient. But I believed that she was kind, too, and wanted the best for everyone. She was my friend.

"Did anyone tell you what she did to Maura?" Kim snorted.

I shook my head. I remembered Bronwyn's story of how Kim had tried to sneak her friend Maura into Metropolitan under a false application, but I thought it best to pretend I had no idea who Maura was.

"I met this woman Maura at a work function," Kim said. "She asked me for a reference for Metropolitan. I said sure. Maura had just been told that she was going to be promoted to partner in her banking firm. The bank was holding back on making the promotion official for bookkeeping purposes, because it was more tax-efficient to wait until the beginning of the following year. I told her to go ahead and tell the school she was a partner because it would be too complicated to explain. Then Bronwyn found out and reported her to the school. The school called the bank, and the bank, thinking it was the IRS, insisted that she wasn't a partner. So Maura's kid had her Metropolitan acceptance withdrawn."

She shook her head and exhaled. "I think Bronwyn will do anything to eliminate the competition."

"Are you *sure* Bronwyn meant to eliminate her?" I asked. Perhaps this was just another misunderstanding.

"Oh, yeah, she was *proud* of it," Kim said, rolling her eyes impatiently. "You know, she really thinks she owns the school."

Kim looked at me searchingly. "Really . . . she thinks she *owns* it."

"What do you mean?" I asked, sensing she was holding something back.

"I've looked at the auction accounts. You know Bronwyn is in charge of the budget for the event. She's the only one authorized to pay for big-ticket items."

"Yes . . ."

"So I looked up some of the bills she's been putting against the auction account. It turns out she's been using the money for stuff that doesn't have much to do with catering."

"Like what?"

"Like a crocodile bag from Fendi. Have you ever priced those things? They cost around twenty thousand bucks. This is not cheap stuff."

I sucked in some air. Was Bronwyn dressing herself at the school's expense? I couldn't believe it. I'd never seen her wear ostentatious designer gear—she tended to favor the "stealth wealth" look: classically cut clothing in expensive yet understated materials. And yet much of Bronwyn's behavior, I realized, was now inexplicable.

"But why would she do that?" I shook my head. "I mean, Bronwyn can afford to buy herself anything she wants." A new sense of dread started to color my thoughts. My shame over having taken Bronwyn's side against Kim was fresh in my mind, and now Kim was trying to get me to side with her against Bronwyn? It really was like being in ninth grade with Erin and Jennie all over again.

Kim leaned closer and whispered, "You know, I've heard through the grapevine that Bronwyn's husband is taking some hits in his career. People say he often goes AWOL. I wouldn't be surprised if he's being pushed out the door. You know, when these bankers go down, they go down in flames. They've usually built up so many overheads that when the bonus doesn't come in, they lose everything—the second house, the boat, the Ferrari, the private jet, everything."

"Are you sure?" I asked incredulously. "Bronwyn acts like she's married to the Rock of Gibraltar." I frowned. If Kim was going to accuse Bronwyn of theft, she really needed proof.

"If we could get into her files, I bet we could prove it in a second," Kim said frankly. "I think she's become a kind of megalomaniac. She probably doesn't think of it as theft. She just figures she owns the school. She gets to decide who gets in, who gets kicked out. Can't you tell she's a complete control freak?"

I nodded grimly. She had a point there.

We paused. I chewed on my salad while my mind teemed with unsavory thoughts.

"I'm sure if she knew what was going on with Eric," Kim said, breaking the silence, "she'd put it in the school newsletter."

She gave me a pleading look. She seemed so vulnerable.

"You know, for a while, they even had me worrying about Jake," she confided quietly. "He's always been such a good kid. But then I thought, *What if they're right? What if Jake's upset over what's happening with his father?* He knows his dad isn't well; what kid *isn't* going to be disturbed by that? Every time he threw a little fit, in the back of my mind, I started to think, *What if he* did *do it? What if Jake killed that hamster?*"

I knew exactly what she was talking about. I realized that every parent of a three-year-old has the same thought at one time or another: *Is there something clinically wrong with my child? Is she destined for a life of crime? Or is it me? Am I a bad parent?*

"It's all about Harrison," Kim said fiercely.

I demurred. I saw how easily I had bought into the idea of Jake as a killer. Now that I knew better, I didn't want to start blaming anybody else's kid. Then again, Snowflake was dead. I remembered the contorted neck, the blank, unblinking stare. And I knew in my heart that it was no accident.

"Look, I feel sorry for Harrison," said Kim. "But Bronwyn is a menace. She's covering up for him by trying to pin the blame on someone else's kid."

"You think Harrison . . . ?"

She gave me a surprised, "Oh, please!" look. "Come on, everybody knows. Why do you think Bronwyn has appointed herself the Committee Queen? That's what women *do* when there is something wrong with their kid! They make themselves indispensable to the school so their kid can't get kicked out!"

I tried to defend Bronwyn, but only halfheartedly. What Kim

had to say was starting to ring true. Bronwyn's casual manner always seemed a little forced. The image of her closing the computer frantically on Harrison's schedule came to my mind. Slowly, awkwardly, I was starting to take sides against her.

"But how do you know?" I asked, still trying to hedge my bets.

"Look," Kim whispered, leaning in close to me. "Betty told me she heard through the nanny grapevine that Bronwyn has been going to this parenting specialist. She's been going two, maybe even three times a week for a year at least. I know it's none of my business, but I think Harrison is troubled. I mean, I feel sorry for him and I hope he gets the help he needs. But I can't let Jake take the blame! Or Anna!"

"It's true that Bronwyn talks to a psychiatrist," I said, thinking aloud. "Some doctor named Dan. But she said she only spoke to him about Jake. . . ."

"What?" Kim shrieked. "She's talking to a psychiatrist about my kid? That is disgusting! So what did this Dr. Dan say about Jake?"

I tried to fudge my way around the subject, but Kim was relentless. I realized there was no way out. She wouldn't rest until I told her.

"She claims that Jake has something called APD. It's where kids can't identify with animals. . . ."

"What a bitch!" Kim exploded. Then she stopped. We looked at each other, and we both had the same thought.

"Don't you see?" she said. "She's got a diagnosis for her own kid, and she's trying to pass it off on my son!"

I sat back, trying to put it all together. Had Bronwyn really been so calculating? Suddenly, it made sense. Harrison was a

problem, and she and her perfect husband with their perfect marriage in their perfect house couldn't tolerate having a problem. I
thought about Bronwyn's spotless kitchen, her army of servants,
her children's hyperengineered lives. Of course Bronwyn did it!
She was a control freak! I mean, what kind of fanatic actually fol-
lows a Martha Stewart recipe down to the last cranberry and then
picks out the cranberries?

"Harrison murdered Snowflake!" I gasped. "And Bronwyn's
been trying to cover up! She's been using me. . . ."

"At least we know what we're up against," Kim said, nodding
grimly.

She looked at me. "You'd better be careful, Laura. I'm used to
fighting. But if Bronwyn can't take me down, she's going to turn
on you."

I sat in silence for a while. I remembered Bronwyn's last conversation with Lloyd.

"She'll do anything," I said, thinking aloud. "She's desperate to
get in with Jeffrey and Eve. You know, she and Lloyd are buying
one of those Royal Villas on Iguana Cay."

Kim's eyes popped open with shock.

Just then, I felt someone's gaze boring into me from outside. I
glanced up through the large window of Bubby's. I saw a pair of
eyes darting between Kim and me, a face twisted with shock and
anger, and lips soundlessly taking the shape of an "Oh! My! God!"

"Bronwyn!" I blurted out involuntarily.

But in a flash she was gone.

Chapter 12

Georgie, Porgie, pudding pie
Kissed the girls and made them cry

"Do you have your membership card?" the young freckled woman at the entrance to Happy Land asked me in a bored voice.

"I'm just here with my friend. . . ." I started to explain.

"That'll be thirty-five dollars for a single adult."

I reached for my wallet, but Kim came to my rescue. She had arrived for our rendezvous with a suitcase at her side. As usual, she had a thousand other things to do, and she was scheduled to fly to Houston that very afternoon. "The main investors in my fund are oilmen," she had explained. "They're the only ones who understand the commodities derivatives markets I trade in. The only problem is I've got to go down and shoot wild ducks with them every now and then, just to prove I'm a man."

"You should see me in my hunting gear," she continued. "When I look in the mirror, even I get scared of me."

Kim turned to the Happy Land receptionist, flashed her family membership card, and said, "She's, er, my new nighttime babysitter. I need to introduce her to Betty."

The freckled woman looked at me suspiciously but waved us in. We went through the turnstile and ducked into the locker room to remove our shoes.

The one time I had taken Anna to Happy Land, when she was two, she had come down with a cold a few days later, and I found the excursion so wearying, not to mention pricey, that I had vowed never to return. But it was one of the few indoor play spaces for kids downtown, and there were always enough customers to keep tussles continuously breaking out over the animal seesaw.

The main play area was as noisy as an airport terminal on spring break. Squeals and cries bounced off the ceiling and ricocheted across the colorfully painted walls of the loft space, which was tricked out with prefab playground equipment. On the worn green Astroturf that covered the floor, toddlers argued over toy cars and bouncy balls in primary colors. Most of them were attended by bored-looking nannies, who congregated on the benches. There was a café in the back selling nutritionally vacuous staples of contemporary children's diets such as juice boxes and Goldfish crackers.

We found Jake in the "swimming pool" made up of thousands of blue and green spongy balls. His nanny, Betty, was on a bench nearby. She was deep in conversation with Bernadette, Bronwyn's nanny. I looked around quickly and spied Bronwyn's daughter, Tess. She was sitting by one of the plastic dollhouse structures, perfectly groomed in a plaid, rather old-fashioned-looking dress with a white cardigan sweater over it.

When Jake spotted his mother, his face lit up, and he squirmed across the sea of foam to give her a hug. While Kim lavished affection on her boy, I approached Bernadette.

"Hello," I said. She smiled and greeted me; clearly she remembered me from the dinner at Bronwyn's loft a few nights earlier.

"So, is Bronwyn home?" I asked. "Er, I left something important at her place. I was hoping to stop by and pick it up."

"She's busy all afternoon," Bernadette replied. "At the hairdresser. She never gets back before five p.m."

Kim and I exchanged glances. This was our cue. It was a reckless idea, but we were determined to carry through with our plan.

"Oh, no," I said, trying for a tone of disappointment and panic. "It's just . . . I need my medication. I mean, I really, really need it."

I squinted my eyes a bit and hunched over slightly, hoping to convey the message that I was suffering from some unspecified and potentially unsavory illness.

Bernadette looked from Kim to me. Kim widened her eyes somberly. Then she looked at Betty, who nodded wordlessly to Bernadette.

"Why don't you just run over—it's only two blocks away," Bernadette said, fishing the keys to Bronwyn's apartment out of her purse.

"Thanks, Bernadette, we'll bring them back in a few minutes," Kim said, holding the keys tightly in her fist. And we sprang into action without a moment's hesitation.

* * *

Kim took the Aeron chair at the desk. I pulled a leather-topped stool next to her and examined some files as she hammered away at the keyboard. In the taxi, on the way down to Happy Land, this hacking expedition had seemed justified. Now, from the walls, a dozen Bronwyns and Lloyds beamed at us from their strategically placed wedding photographs, and I felt a little guilty and more than a little foolish. Above the computer keyboard, a wide, flat screen on the wall was lit up with Kim's work on the computer.

If we could find the right spreadsheet on Bronwyn's computer, we figured we would have the proof we needed to convict her of sticking her own purchases to the auction account.

The computer had been on when we got there, as though someone had just stepped away for a few moments.

"I'm really not sure we should be doing this," I said to Kim nervously as I scanned Bronwyn's desktop. I felt strong twinges of guilt about being in Bronwyn's home. My conscience kept stealing into the room. I had never stooped so low. In the back of my mind, I knew I was guilty of something. *But of what? Breaking and entering? Snooping?* Had I become another one of New York's cutthroat moms, willing to do anything to get her child ahead? In fact, I had. But I was far from willing to admit it to myself.

Kim looked a little unsure, too. Then she drew her lips taut. "We have to do it for the children," she said. "Remember, this is about more than a couple discrepancies on the auction budget. We need to protect our kids from Harrison. And Harrison needs help."

I nodded grimly. With a hamster killer on the loose in my

daughter's classroom, this was no time to get squeamish. Besides, when Bronwyn had invited me to her house, she had even said I could use her computer for school business anytime. I thought about how she had misled me, how she had insinuated that Kim was some sort of monster—Kim, who was trying to raise her boy and stay true to a husband who had let her down so badly! I shuddered. I remembered, too, how coldly Bronwyn and Lloyd had treated their own son when he misbehaved the night I came to dinner. Perhaps that was the reason for his acting out. *Poor Harrison,* I thought.

As Kim flicked through Bronwyn's files on the screen, she paused every now and then and *tsk*ed with dissatisfaction. Once or twice, I caught her glancing at me sideways. I knew she still carried within her a grain of suspicion. She had confided so much in me, and I knew that a part of her would never be comfortable with that. I wanted to reassure her, tell her that I understood. But I figured she was the kind of woman who needed time, not words.

"God, her spreadsheets are a disaster!" Kim fumed, clicking through Bronwyn's files. "Everything looks perfect when you open it, but once you look in the individual cells, all you see is garbage! Instead of adding things up with formulas, she must just take out a pocket calculator and put in the summation herself. If she worked for me, I'd fire her!"

"How incompetent!" I said, nodding gravely. Of course, I had no idea what Kim was talking about.

She took me through Bronwyn's spreadsheets to make her point. As even I could see, Bronwyn had been meticulous in her choice of fonts and bold and italics for the labels of her accounts. But within each little box, where the actual dollar figures were supposed to appear, there was just a jumble of numbers.

We were getting nowhere fast. Trying to track the missing money in Bronwyn's jerry-rigged files was like fishing for a missing baby sock in huge load of laundry.

"Let's go through the history," Kim said impatiently. She started looking through the record of programs and files.

An Internet browser window flashed open. Suddenly, the wide, flat screen on the wall zoomed in on a big-breasted blonde woman, naked except for a ten-gallon hat and cowboy chaps.

"I've been naughty!" read the flashing banner. *"So spank me!"*

The woman turned and raised her rear end, and moans of excitement started to issue through the computer speakers.

"God, these pop-ups ought to be illegal!" Kim said, rolling her eyes and lunging for the volume knob.

She tried to click off the window, but then another one popped up. "Well-*cum* back!" it flashed. We'd been automatically logged on to a new site. This time it was a video reel of two women writhing in simulated ecstasy. "CALL 1-800-123-4567! Teach Keri and Randi a lesson!" read the header.

I couldn't help giggling. Kim snorted as she shut down the window.

It came right back up. "Bad girls like us need to be punished!" the screen flashed. Kim looked at me uncertainly. "I'm not sure this is a pop-up. . . . It's coming from the history. . . ." she said, looking at me mystified. "This is Bronwyn's computer, isn't it? Do you think maybe she is into this kind of stuff?"

"You never know," I said, staring at the screen. "Maybe she and Lloyd have a wild sex life." I shrugged. "Should we be jealous?"

"Wouldn't it mess up her hair?" Kim said.

I tried to picture Bronwyn undressing for an orgy. In my mind, she was taking way too long to unbutton her sweater.

Suddenly, an instant message popped up on the screen.

"hey babe! im lonely!" It came from Randi.

Kim looked at me. "Do you think maybe 'Randi' is her hairdresser?"

"keri needs a LICKIN! make that a WHIPPIN! r u cummin over?"

Now Kim and I were alarmed. I saw a vertical line appear on Kim's brow. It had been amusing at first, but this was disturbing.

"Maybe it was Jared, the computer guy," I said, remembering that Bronwyn had called her computer guy to fix the machine. "Or some sort of porn virus."

"Anyway, it's none of our business," Kim mumbled in agreement, shutting down the browser.

She looked at her watch in frustration. "Damn, we haven't found anything," she whispered, looking at me uncomfortably. "And I've got to leave now if I'm going to return those keys to Bernadette and still make that flight to Houston on time."

She got up and hurriedly gathered her bag. "Why don't you stay here a few more minutes?" she suggested. "Just make sure to close the door behind you; it's the kind that locks automatically." After suggesting a few search tips I could try on my own in the time remaining, she exited the apartment.

I dragged the cursor around the screen, unsure of where to

look. The pointer settled on Bronwyn's scheduling software. Shamefacedly repeating to myself, *I'm doing this for the kids,* I clicked on the program. Immediately, a window opened showing Bronwyn's schedule for that day. I checked my watch: 1:50 p.m. I looked on her schedule. The 1:00 p.m. slot was allocated to a Dr. Daniel Forest, M.D., LDSW.

That didn't sound like a hairdresser. Then I remembered Bronwyn talking about her psychiatrist friend Dan. I remembered his alleged insights into Jake's psychological problems, the APD diagnosis. All of a sudden, it was obvious. Dan wasn't a friend at all, I realized. He was her shrink. Or maybe Harrison's.

I opened the Internet browser and Googled Dr. Daniel Forest to see if I could find out more about him.

To my alarm, the window with Randi and Keri popped back up. The instant messenger flashed on.

"ahh cum on don't be shy," Randi said. "r u punishing me?"

I stared dumbly at the screen. Somebody was really there! An actual person! "I don't want to know about this," I mumbled to myself.

Suddenly, I thought: *Maybe I do.* None of this was making any sense—not Kim's paranoia, not Bronwyn's hostility, and especially not the fact that I had somehow turned into a trespasser and a snoop. Maybe whoever was out there would offer some kind of a clue. I decided to reply.

"hey," I typed tentatively back to Randi.

"i knew you were there, lloydie-floydie!" Randi shot back. "r u lonely? im at the townhouse til 2 a.m. u cummin?"

I gasped. Of course. It was Lloyd. I felt overwhelmed with the burden of this knowledge. *Should I tell Bronwyn? Or did she already know?* It was my own fault that I found myself here in this predicament. I was a burglar, a schemer, a fink. I wanted to run, to find my daughter, play in the grass, and forget everything I'd learned.

I closed off Randi's window and found the results of my Web search. Dr. Daniel Forest, I learned, was a prominent family therapist. One link brought me to a lecture he had delivered at the annual conference of the American Psychiatric Association. It was titled: Sex Addiction: The New Epidemic.

I didn't have to tell Bronwyn anything, I realized. I looked at the wedding pictures of Bronwyn and Lloyd that covered the walls. I knew now why she had sometimes seemed so strangely tense. She must have carried this burden for a long time. Her first marriage had been a disaster, and her second was a fraud. A woman like Bronwyn—controlling, yes, but also empathetic— would probably end up blaming herself. I wanted to find her and talk to her, tell her it was all right, that it wasn't her fault, that she could stop pretending.

I began to wonder about Harrison, too. Dr. Forest clearly wasn't a specialist in child psychology. So he probably wasn't treating Harrison. Had Kim and I jumped the gun?

I was so absorbed in my thoughts that I didn't hear the noise of the door opening.

"Hey, Laura, what brings you here?" I heard Lloyd say in a friendly, casual voice. I started and looked up. Lloyd was standing at the doorway of the office. He was wearing faded jeans and a sweater, as though dressed for a weekend with the kids. I simply couldn't connect the image of the sandy-haired husband and father standing in front of me with lloydie-floydie at Randi's town house. It all seemed so surreal.

"Oh, uh, hey," I stammered, hastily shutting down the computer and jumping to my feet. "I was just, uh, uploading some files for the, uh, school auction, you know." I desperately prayed that Bronwyn hadn't had a chance to tell him that she and I were no longer speaking. "What are you doing at home in the middle of the day?"

Did I really just ask a guy what he's doing in his own house? I wondered. He didn't seem to notice.

"They gave us the day off at work. Hah, hah!" he said, laughing to himself.

"That's great," I said. "I'm sorry, uh, were you on the computer? I hope I didn't mess up you—"

"No problem," he said, stepping past me and sitting down at the Aeron chair. He glanced at his watch. "Well, I'd better get back to business."

"Yeah, um, thanks, nice to see you," I said nervously.

He gave me a nod. I withdrew from the office and slunk out of the apartment as quickly as I could. When I got to the street, I started running and didn't stop until long after I had turned the corner.

When I was out of breath, I found myself passing the Odeon. I needed time to think about everything I had learned. I turned from the noisy thoroughfare of West Broadway and wandered over to the quiet cobblestones of Laight Street. I glimpsed into the converted industrial warehouses that rose on either side of me. At one time, they had housed factories and cow carcasses. Now they were luxury lofts and high-end furniture stores. Groups of husky-looking men in business suits were walking in the direction of Wall Street, probably on their way back from lunch. I had about fifteen minutes before I had to pick Anna up from school. I knew I wouldn't be able to feel any peace of mind until I had spoken to Bronwyn, though I had no idea what I would say to her. She'd be furious that I'd broken into her house. But I wanted to tell her how wrong we'd both been about Kim. And how wrong Kim and I had been about her. Mainly, I wanted to comfort her. I knew she needed a shoulder to cry on.

My call went through. I heard her pick up, but she said nothing. I knew she would have seen my name on the caller ID.

"Bronwyn, I—"

"*YOU* had *LUNCH* with *KIM*!" she spat. "After all I did for you! Don't ever, *EVER* call me."

She hung up.

I waited for a moment, then redialed. I got a message indicating that she had blocked all calls from my number.

Chapter 13

Five for silver, six for gold
Seven for a secret, ne'er to be told

I stared at the Sun & Frolic memo and willed myself to invent a marketing campaign theme. I had exactly one hour and forty-three minutes of free time remaining. *Now!* I told myself. *Now you must work!* But my brain was not responding.

I had Richard to thank for the hour and forty-three minutes. He alone could persuade Anna to walk. My daughter's identity as an infant cat-cow had taken a new and bizarre twist. She wasn't walking. More precisely, she wasn't walking whenever I was around. Instead, she'd lie on the floor and insist that cat-cows need to be carried by their mommies.

I had called Metropolitan that morning and told them that Anna had a cold. Then I had taken her to the pediatrician and demanded to know if there might be a physiological reason for Anna's refusal to walk. The doctor examined Anna carefully and announced that there was nothing physically wrong with her. She then turned to me and whispered that I might want to have her evaluated by a specialist in pediatric mental health.

So I loaded Anna up in the stroller and wheeled her over to our therapist's office for an emergency session. I deliberately misspelled Anna's surname as we registered, vainly hoping that the episode would not make it onto her permanent school record. The therapist scratched his beard while Anna told him about the special needs of cat-cows. He then mumbled something to me about "regression" and "testing her power" and how "it was all part of growing up." He advised me to give her "more breathing room." I was to leave her in the care of her daddy as much as possible.

When Richard heard the news, he grumbled that he was already late delivering a paper on the Cartesian worldview. Nonetheless, he came home for lunch and lured Anna into the hallway. "Cat-cows learn to walk on two legs before they walk on all four," I heard him reason with her though the bedroom/office door.

"When I'm big, I'm gonna walk on four legs," she agreed.

"Let's go to the park and see if we can find other cat-cows."

"No! There are only dog-cows in the park."

"Even better. Dog-cows are *very* friendly."

"Hurray!"

"We'll be back in one hour and forty-five minutes," Richard said in a loud voice for my benefit. And they were off.

Recently, Carter, my boss, had taken to sending fake friendly e-mail reminders about the project. "Can't wait to have your input!" he'd gush, by which he meant: "Where the hell is your stuff?"

So far, I had managed to keep Carter at bay with a series of cryptic replies. I led him to believe that I was in the midst of creative agonies over the final details of the project, and that it would be only a matter of moments before I sacrificed my artistic integrity by showing it to him and thereby relinquishing control of my opus. In fact, I hadn't even started.

Didn't these people understand that sending your daughter to preschool is a full-time job?

As if to prove the point, just then the phone rang, and I heard the familiar voice of the sand vendor.

"So, lady, you finally figure out what kinda sand you want?" he asked without preface.

"This is for the *Metropolitan* auction," I said. "You better send over the finest, most expensive damn sand you've got."

"Well, *excuse me,* Miss *Metropolitan.* I didn't know you were so *la-dee-dah*! So I guess you'll be wanting the superfine sand, scented, *with* pebbles *and* shells *and* artificial dessicated crabs?"

"Whatever! Just send enough for one fake island!"

"See you there, Miss *Metropolitan.*" He slammed down the phone.

Sun and Frolic. Sun and Frolic. I repeated the words like a mantra. I stared at the memo of agreement my boss had hammered out with the client late one night at some godforsaken bar in Chicago. It didn't help that the whole thing had been written in Arial font.

I mean, that's the default font on most e-mail. It says, hey, I just typed this bureaucratic bullshit in, and I haven't even started thinking about it! But, really, it's a great hotel, 2000 rooms, 10 mins from full svc airport, white sandy beaches, great nightlife, a great value for economy-conscious segment.

I decided that the problem was that Carter had contaminated my imagination with his metaphorical description of cardboard boxes on the beach. I concentrated on getting rid of them. I saw dark, gray clouds gathering over Providenciales. My inner meteorologist told me it was hurricane season and a tropical storm was gathering force. The storm grew and grew, swallowing up the blue sky around it. The clouds bunched up into the shape of a wolf, and the wolf said, "Hey, little island, I'm going to huff and puff and blow your tacky cardboard shacks right into the Caribbean! Hah!"

Sun and Frolic: You'll be blown away!

I put my head in my arms on the desk, close to weeping tears of frustration. I was getting nowhere! I looked up at my fantasy island scene and saw a clear, sunny patch on the horizon, a place where the skies were always blue, the water was an unending stretch of rippling turquoise, and smiling attendants were proffering chilled glasses of hibiscus tea and full-body ayurvedic massages. I realized I was looking at Iguana Cay.

In the past two days, the news about Iguana Cay had electrified the moms and dads of Metropolitan. Discussions of the tropical paradise filled the hallways of the school. All but the most inert parents understood the proposition. Iguana Cay was everything to which they had ever aspired. It was the sunny, utopian answer to all the realities of life in the dark canyons of lower Manhattan. It was going to be a place to "get away from it all"—and to do it together with all the people who *mattered*.

Members of the Iguana Club would spend their holidays rubbing Calypsos with the likes of Jeffrey and Eve. Rumor had it that the entire board of Holyfield was signing up for the venture, too. Plus, by buying early and sight unseen through the school auction, savvy parents would have an opportunity to come in at a discount, before the public clambered in and drove up the prices even higher. "The Turks and Caicos is the hottest market in the Caribbean!" I heard them whisper to each other at the drop-off. "It's the new Saint Barths!"

It was starting to look like Kim had negotiated an excellent deal for Metropolitan and its parents. The base prices she had agreed on with Jeffrey now looked to many people like bargains. Parents would be able to bid above the base prices, thereby giving Metropolitan a lavish commission, and they would still be buying low. Their Caribbean vacation homes would end up costing less than comparable properties on other, less desirable islands and might even earn them a profit if they decided to resell after a year or two.

Telling myself it was research, I closed the Sun & Frolic memo and went to the Iguana Cay website. Jeffrey, or more likely his assistant, Bruce, had recently put the promotional slide show online with accompanying text. I clicked through the pictures. There was the same smiling Caribbean youth, the glistening bowl of fruit, the white clay villas swathed in bougainvillea. I paused. There was the picture of three palm trees on a sandbar, surrounded by ocean, with a sailboat in the distance. It looked comfortable and familiar, and for some reason I felt sure I would feel at home there. In fact, I felt like it was as much a part of my natural environment as the desk I was sitting at. This place belonged to me, I thought indignantly. How dare Jeffrey sell it to a bunch of . . . arrivistes!

Fuming, I pictured the parents of Metropolitan cavorting in the sunshine, playing volleyball on the beach with their children, relaxing with martinis at sunset, chatting about life at Holyfield, then, in the languorous evening, quietly . . . swapping partners. Jeffrey came up with a knowing look and tapped me gently on the arm. As I got up, I caught Bronwyn's eye. She had obviously been crying all night. Suddenly, I felt a dark wind. Lloyd was standing at the door, a telltale smirk on his lips. I closed the website.

I was just torturing myself. I'd never get to see Iguana Cay. And it was useless for my purposes as a copywriter to even think about it. No matter how hard it tried, Sun & Frolic could never be Iguana Cay. From whatever angle you shot the grim, white matchbox grid of motel rooms, you just couldn't make it look like a private villa draped in purple flowers with a landscaped garden and an infinity-edge plunge pool. Sun & Frolic promotional literature wisely avoided interior shots, which I was sure would reveal tacky upholstery and standard-issue porcelain in the bathrooms. Iguana Cay was picture-perfect. Even the bathrooms were spectacular, as I recalled, vaguely remembering slides of marble countertops and elegant, claw-foot bathtubs.

Unable to resist, I clicked on the Iguana Cay website to have another look. Yes, there were the bathrooms. I pictured myself clad in a tasteful but alluring tropical cotton peignoir, brushing my hair luxuriantly in the mirror. The smell of complimentary expensive scented bath products was all around me. Another figure was entering the reflection behind me. It was . . . Lloyd. *Yuk!* I couldn't erase him from my mind. I pictured him there in the bathroom, a laptop on his knees. *But wait! There was Richard! Looking over his shoulder! At Randi!*

My thoughts were suddenly disrupted by a new and disturbing suspicion. How did I know my husband wasn't leading a secret life, too? What if Bronwyn and I had more in common than I thought? It was hard to imagine . . . but then again, I would never have imagined that Amy, his college girlfriend, was any kind of threat. In a panic, I decided to investigate the history on our computer.

I scanned through the list of recently viewed sites. To my relief, I found page after page on dreary seventeenth-century philosophers: Descartes, Leibniz, Spinoza . . . *There ought to be a law against this kind of stuff on the Internet,* I thought. *It could bore you to death!*

Okay, so Richard wasn't a lascivious creep like Lloyd. In fact, maybe that was his problem. He was too innocent, naïve, an easy mark for sharks like Amy. The same sense of guilt and foolishness I had felt when cyber-snooping at Bronwyn's house returned. Plus, I was getting hungry.

I walked into the kitchen and opened the fridge, but it was nearly empty. We needed groceries, I told myself, glad to have something so practical to do. Richard had recently set up an account with an Internet grocer, so I punched the Web address into my computer and went to their website.

Quickly, I clicked on the basics: bread, eggs, milk, fruit, and vegetables. When I came to the checkout, however, I realized

Richard had failed to inform me of the password. I hit the "Forgot your password?" link, and the clue to the mystery was sent to Richard's e-mail, which he always left on, usually to my annoyance. It seemed like whenever I got into a writing groove, a little voice would announce, "You've got mail!" And during the two seconds it took to log him out, the muse would inevitably depart.

At least for once, Richard's habit of leaving everything in the house in whatever state it happened to be when he lost interest in it was a convenience, I thought to myself, opening his incoming-mail folder.

Then I saw it. An email from Amy2534@hotmail.com. Scarcely able to breathe, I scanned down the list and saw a half-dozen more. Intentionally giving myself no time to count to ten, I opened one.

Great to see you the other day!

"What other day?" I barked at the computer. And what was with the pretentious font?

It's been so long, and I have so much to tell you. Let's talk soon. I hope L is well.

L! So I was reduced to an initial! She'd lopped off the last four letters of my name! My "aura"! She wanted to eliminate me!

Autumn on MacDougal Street has hardly been the season of mellow fruitfulness, as Keats might have expounded. As I meander through the concrete jungle we call the metropolis, I am enveloped in the heartache of solitude. Alone I am, alone as I walk the mean streets and peer into the faces of my fellow urban dwellers, hoping for kindness but finding nothing but darkness and despair. Alone, I tend to my hopes and my dreams like Voltaire to his garden. My tender Anna is the one consolation in this land-scape of desolation.

Not only was she a husband stealer, she was a criminally bad writer!

I opened another e-mail from the conniving witch.

The harvest of this season has been the bitter-tasting fruit of knowledge. W is so unyielding. His ideals are so different from mine; our pathways are so divergent. Once I had thought we were star-crossed lovers; now we are but strangers in the night, passing ships whose horns sound mournfully into the bitter wind, never to be answered. As I reflect upon my life in the mid-night hour, I realize now that you were my one true love, a beacon of light that shone strong and true, but was obscured by the gathering stormclouds of life's vicissitudes. Fate has been cruel to me. Has it been cruel to you too, my friend? When we are together, I sense something unspoken. Perhaps true love needs no words, it is as timeless as the winds. I savor the memories of our moment in my mind's eye like a fine cognac, always improving with age. Do you remember our senior-year seminar on Abelard?

So it was true! She was trying to ditch her lard-ball husband and latch onto Richard. Right under my nose! And she was doing it with a clutch of mixed metaphors and awful clichés! How could Richard actually fall for this?

I was shaking with anger and hurt. What now?

Numbly, I opened the e-mail from the online grocery store.

"Welcome back," it read. "Your password is: Abelard."

Abelard. The seminar Richard had shared with Amy!

I got up in a haze. My life was over.

I suddenly felt dizzy. Holding on to the desk to steady myself, I looked around at our apartment: the shelves stuffed with dog-eared books and stacks of old magazines; the framed posters; the collection of Dean Martin on vinyl I had given to Richard for Valentine's Day. All lies.

My mind turned to Anna. What would become of her? Would she be one of those children who sees her father once a week, dropped off and picked up by hostile parents? Or would Richard fight me for custody? I shuddered when I realized that if I lost my job—an increasingly likely prospect, given my inability to meet my deadlines—maybe he could win a custody battle and take her away. *Anna!*

I was too shocked to cry. I was like a passenger in a crashing plane who understands what is happening but just keeps watching the bad in-flight movie on the overhead projector, too resigned to what is coming to bother moving.

After a while, my mental paralysis began to make me physically restless. There was no home for me, here or in Iguana Cay. I got up, located my keys, and walked out the door. I didn't want to be in the apartment when Richard and Anna got back. I just couldn't bear to face him.

Chapter 14

Peter, Peter, pumpkin eater
Had a wife and couldn't keep her

It was a gray afternoon, a gray so bright it was almost white. Richard had taken Anna to school. After my discoveries and my walk the day before, I had returned home in the early evening with just enough energy to bury myself in Anna's bedtime ritual. I still had no idea what to do and needed time to strategize. Today, I had again found myself pacing the sidewalks of TriBeCa. But I hadn't come up with any answers.

Who can I talk to? I asked myself. *Who will listen without judging?* My mind flitted to Bronwyn. In spite of her shortcomings, I missed our friendship. But seeing as how she absolutely refused to answer my calls, I certainly couldn't talk to her. Then I thought of Dominique. Several days had passed since we had exchanged incoherent messages. Dominique was like that: flighty, and a little hard to reach. But somehow, I felt Dominique would understand. There was so much I had to tell her, about Kim, Bronwyn, and . . . myself. True, she was locked in her own world. But she was honest, too. She would tell me the truth, whether I wanted to hear it or not.

Was Dominique at Bloom? I wondered. My feet had taken me to within a few blocks of the restored cast-iron building on Duane Street, and I hurried over the remaining distance. The cool Brit receptionist at the front desk recognized me, I could tell. But she didn't acknowledge our previous exchange, and simply greeted me with a frosty "May I help you?"

I asked if I could go in to look for Dominique.

"I'm sorry, but the club is for members only."

I reminded her that Dominique had put me on her permanent guest list.

She shuffled some papers. "I'm sorry, but I don't see any evidence of that."

"Evidence?" My voice rose.

"I'm going to have to ask you to leave," she snapped, her eyes steely. "If you raise your voice in here again, I will call security."

Had Dominique iced me, too? Or was it Bronwyn who had filled her ears with poison? As I stood there pondering the possibilities, three women stepped out of the elevator. I recognized them instantly.

"Everybody is getting one!" I heard Serena's mom say as she passed by the receptionist.

"I know," Pearl Necklace said. "We're putting our deposit in now!"

"Peak season at the best places in the Turks and Caicos is

booked, like, five years in advance," Serena's mom continued. "This way, we can hop down last-minute!"

"Yeah, we can always charter a boat to Parrot Cay for yoga classes," said Pearl Necklace.

"Emilio had his heart set on the *Sex and the City* part," Pilar chimed in. "Now he also wants to get an Imperial Estate."

"Wow! Just like Emilio, always wanting to make a splash! Hee, hee."

"Hey, did you hear Dominique say she's going for one of the Deluxe Bungalows?"

Dominique? I could hardly believe it. So she had joined the sorority, too. As the ladies swooshed past me, Pilar and I exchanged glances. Her eyes narrowed in recognition, but she didn't acknowledge me. *What a bunch of Heathers,* I said to myself. But it still stung as sharply as though I'd been slapped. The three had walked past me as though I were a potted plant. This was worse than ninth grade.

The receptionist looked at me with a sneer. I turned my back and walked out the door.

Dazed, I again began to wander the streets. Now I was truly alone. The Metropolitan mothers had lined up against me. Richard was in the process of leaving me for Amy. Even Anna, my sweet, astonishing Anna, was growing out of reach. My old buddies from prenatal yoga had scattered to follow their own paths. And Kim, my one new friend in this harsh, confusing world, was out of town on a mission to kill wild ducks.

Eventually, I found myself in Battery Park, overlooking the Hudson River. Full of self-pity, I sat on a wooden bench and watched the brackish water lapping against the docks, trying to find some tranquility in the soothing sound of the current. But the wail of fire engines behind me intruded. *There must be a better place than this,* I thought. I closed my eyes and pictured myself lying on my fantasy beach on Iguana Cay, sipping the juice of a freshly opened coconut, holding hands with . . . Jeffrey.

The passing sirens receded, and the fantasy started to gather some force. Yes, Jeffrey and I were lying arm in arm in the sun-warmed sand. But this time, Anna was building a sandcastle at our feet. I flashed on the picture featured in the Iguana Cay slideshow with the three palm trees on a sandbar. One palm tree for each of us, I decided: Anna, Jeffrey, and me.

The vision fortified me. Maybe it foretold my fate. Anna would make it through Metropolitan and then move on—maybe even to Holyfield, I decided. If Richard ran off with Amy, Anna and I would survive. So what if I couldn't afford even the front porch on a bungalow at Iguana Cay? My role was to be the deprived scholarship mom, and I would make the most of it. A divorce would add color to the résumé. It might even qualify me as a "diversity" candidate. And Jeffrey? Was I wrong to think that a certain spark had passed between us that night at the party? Didn't it all make sense in a way—that Richard reconnected with his lost love, Amy, on the same night that the torch of my passion passed on to another?

A mad thought crossed my mind. I should talk to Jeffrey! After all, my daughter was a Forsythe Scholar—we owed our very presence at the school to his generosity. I *had* to fill him in on the brewing school conflicts. It was my duty!

I knew where his home was—it was listed in the school directory. Staple Street, a narrow cobblestone alleyway banked by nineteenth-century warehouses. I would go there, and I would tell him what was happening. Somehow I was sure he would understand. We had exchanged only a few words, and yet there was something between us, wasn't there? He would know in an instant why I had come. Maybe we wouldn't even talk. Maybe he would just wrap his strong arms around me. . . .

I rushed home while there was still time. Anna was at school, and Richard was buried in the library. I rummaged maniacally through the closet, looking for my favorite dress, the one that showed my legs to their best advantage. My legs were the last feature of my body that I was sure still said "hot." My breasts had started to head south after childbirth, and my eyes were permanently baggy from lack of sleep. But running after Anna had kept my thighs firm and shapely.

Then I moved to the bathroom, where I spent fifteen minutes blowing out my hair. I slipped on the dress and vamped for the mirror, daubed some cover-up under my eyes, and dubiously examined the results. A swipe of lipstick, a few strokes of the mascara wand, and I was ready for action.

Outside, the sky was still a bright, painful gray, and the air was thick with humidity. I knew it was only a matter of time before my hair bunched back up into an unruly bush, so I moved along quickly, rehearsing my speech to Jeffrey as I walked. I would show grave concern about the future of the school. I would appear in need of help but not helpless. I wanted to be his lover, not his minion. I thought bitterly of my feckless husband, and I consoled myself with visions of life at the Iguana Club.

"Yes, my first husband . . . gave me the most wonderful daughter imaginable. But his contribution to our family more or less ended with conception," I'd say, my voice steeped in the wisdom of sensual experience, sweeping my arms across the luscious tropical vistas. "I always longed for a deeper and more spiritual union. . . ."

As I approached Jeffrey's place on Staple Street, a few prickly little slivers of reality penetrated my feverish thoughts. What if he wasn't at home? Or worse, what if Eve was? What if Jeffrey was in the middle of a big business deal? What if he simply didn't remember who I was? To make matters worse, despite the marathon blowout session, my hair was starting to frizz.

Suddenly, I felt exposed. I made my way along the cobbled stones of Harrison Street, wondering if any of the other Metropolitan parents who lived nearby might see me and guess my clandestine purpose. I glanced in the windows of Tribeca Pediatrics, then lingered by the other shops, pretending to shop through the windows of Capucine, a high-end boutique for yoga mamas, trying to muster up my courage. As a school benefactor, I reminded myself firmly, Jeffrey deserved to know, and right away, before my hair got any frizzier. There was no turning back. I faced the street, training my sights on the door to Jeffrey's home.

That's when the door swung open.

It was Dominique!

She had a glorious smile on her face, and she looked up at the thick cloud cover as though it was brilliant with sunshine. She was in full gypsy regalia, a feast of color against the somber browns and grays of the street. Necklaces jangling softly, she turned and walked south, in the other direction, toward Duane Street. Apparently, she hadn't spotted me. What was she doing here, coming out of Jeffrey's home just as I was arriving for my secret tryst-to-be? As I watched her walk away, she slung a beautifully crafted crocodile handbag insouciantly over her shoulder.

Even from a distance, I recognized the style. It was a Fendi.

There were the pair of interlocking F's on the handbag's clasp. She might as well have covered herself with hundred-dollar bills taken straight from the Metropolitan auction budget.

I turned and ran in the opposite direction.

Dominique had deceived me! She had fooled us all! Stealing from the school, seducing Jeffrey, it was all just a game to her. She was obviously manipulating everyone around her. *Us Weekly* was wrong! Stars were not just like us! It was too much.

Lost in these thoughts, I nearly slammed into a uniformed nanny pushing a double stroller, but I didn't stop. Little droplets of rain started falling on my face and bare legs. They mixed with the tears streaming down my cheeks. I jogged up Church Street, crossed Canal, and tore through SoHo, dodging the shoppers and tourists that crowded the sidewalks. By the time I got home, it was pouring and I was panting so hard I was gasping for breath.

In my bedroom/office, I ripped off my sodden clothes. I sat down at my desk in my underwear and ran my fingers through my hair. In an hour, it would be one giant frizzball.

When Richard arrived home with Anna, I was curled up in the bed, pretending to sleep.

Anna bounded into the room. She was carrying a new stuffed cat in one hand. When she saw me, her eyes widened in excitement and she skipped over. "I love you so much," I said, reaching out to give my daughter a kiss.

But she eluded my grasp. "Kisses are yucky," she said. "They are made out of spit."

"Oh, okay," I said. "I won't kiss you then. Can I hug you?"

"Mommy, cat-cows sometimes get hungry," Anna replied, ignoring the question.

"I'm sorry, Sweet Pea, Mommy's not feeling well," I told her. "Let Daddy make you dinner tonight."

Seeing her disappointed look, I added, "Why don't you choose some books and I'll read them to you? Daddy can make us dinner."

Richard watched me skeptically for a few moments until I reluctantly turned to him.

"What?" I exhaled, looking at him with tired eyes. "Am I not allowed to get sick?"

"Suit yourself." He shrugged. "Come on, Anna, I'll take you out for pizza."

I let them go.

Chapter 15

The wind, the wind, the wind blows high
The rain comes scattering down the sky

The next morning, it was still raining. I put the clear plastic shield over the stroller. Anna swiftly batted it away. "But mommy, cat-cows like the rain," she said matter-of-factly.

"Cat-cows can get sick if they get wet," I reasoned, putting the shield back down. Anna batted it back up. I glanced out the window. *Just a drizzle,* I told myself. I bundled Anna into an extra sweater, then zipped up her purple butterfly rain jacket.

"Okay, sweetheart, just make sure you keep your hood on. I don't want you catching a cold," I said, leaning close to her and nuzzling her little neck. She smelled so sweet. Part of me wished I didn't have to send her to school at all. I would have liked to spend the day at the zoo, looking at monkeys and penguins. *Tomorrow, we'll play hooky,* I promised myself. But not today. Today, I was on a mission.

At the drop-off, predictably, Anna rolled off the stroller and lay down on the carpeted floor of her classroom.

"Moo-meow," she said. This cat-cow act of hers was clearly gathering steam.

As she rolled from side to side, mooing and meowing, I unzipped her rain jacket and began to wipe her dry. We must have made an interesting sight. But as far as the other mommies present were concerned, I might as well have been the Invisible Disadvantaged Mother. They looked right through me as they nodded greetings to one another. Even the nannies seemed to understand that I was a mommy non grata.

I was pretty sure this was Bronwyn's doing. She had been meticulous in her plans to avoid all contact with me. Aside from blocking my calls, I suspected she was sending her nanny ahead to scout for my presence at the school, just to make sure that we didn't bump into each other. With a few well-chosen words whispered into the cell phone airways of lower Manhattan, she had ensured that my name among the Metropolitan mothers was mud.

Dominique's daughter waltzed past us in the care of her nanny, sniffing at Anna with a precocious form of Gallic disdain.

There, I thought with a flash of insight, *goes Snowflake's murderer!*

Dominique had been so clever, I thought. She had thrown us all off the scent. She had insinuated that Snowflake's killer was one of the boys, feigned indifference about the whole thing, then watched with silent satisfaction as Kim and Bronwyn and I ripped each other apart.

Then, in one final move, she had sealed her victory by joining Bronwyn and Kim in the Iguana Cay investment. It was foolproof. And there was only one possible outcome: The school would eventually let the blame for Snowflake settle on Anna.

Kim was my last remaining hope. But she was still trapped in some godforsaken swamp in eastern Texas, well out of cellular-reception range. Whenever I tried to call, there was no response. And the hope was a dim one. Would Kim really choose to side with me against her future Caribbean neighbors? She was enough of a businesswoman to know I had no leverage. I could never tell the school about Jake's father without feeling that I was betraying James. She had made it this far on her own. Why would she bother going down with my ship when she could just disembark and board a flight to Iguana Cay?

At last, Tori emerged from her classroom and stared at us wordlessly. "Could you help me out here?" I said to her, exasperated by her passivity. Tori may have been pursuing a master's degree in early education, as Sunny had reported, but sometimes it seemed as though she lacked any intuitive grasp of toddler psychology. I picked up my daughter and physically handed her to her teacher, so that Tori was forced to give her some concentrated attention. With Anna's focus diverted, she finally let me leave.

I took a seat on one of the benches along the lobby wall, underneath a Friends of Metropolitan group portrait. I was determined to have a word with Sunny.

It crossed my mind that Bronwyn's or Dominique's insidious rumors might have already reached the school director. I struggled to remember exactly what I had told Dominique about my troubles with Richard. I pictured her chatting idly with Sunny, casually dropping hints about my jealous rages.

How dare she! The outrage boiled up from within. It was so easy for her. Just like buying a fancy handbag on the school's dime. I had to act immediately.

I knocked on Sunny's door. She was hunched over her desk, examining some papers, her large opal pendant dangling over her lap.

"Is everything all right?" she said.

I glanced at the van Gogh flower print above her desk. I could hear the kids talking and laughing in the classroom next door.

"Um, I just thought you should know," I said, "Kim and I have been looking into the auction budget. We think maybe Dominique has been misappropriating some of the auction money. We think she bought an expensive handbag for herself. . . ."

"Oh, dear!" Sunny gasped theatrically. "But are you sure there isn't a misunderstanding here? You know, the stores donate all kinds of gifts to the auction."

"Well," I said, uncertain how far I should push the case.

"Did you check with the store to see who made the purchases?" she asked, a faint look of worry crossing her brow.

"Well, no," I admitted.

"I see."

"I just thought it was something we should pay attention to."

"Point taken! I will look into the matter personally."

She smiled, but her smile seemed to stop before it reached her eyes. She gave me a piercing look.

"In the meantime," she added, "let's keep this conversation our little secret." She pulled an imaginary zipper across her mouth. "You know how these mothers get when the rumors start to fly!"

I nodded and retreated.

On the way home, I tried to convince myself I had done the right thing. But had I? I wasn't sure. Did I really know what made Sunny tick? Her effusive manner had always put me at ease. Now, for the first time, it occurred to me that it was also a kind of a shield. By keeping everyone smiling, I realized, Sunny also managed to keep everyone thinking about themselves, and not her.

In the afternoon, when Richard brought Anna home from school, I was again lying on the bed, trying to make sense of what was happening around me. Richard sat Anna down in front of the TV and popped in a Berenstain Bears video titled *All About Manners*.

"There's some stuff here for you," he said, placing a pile of mail in front of me.

"Thanks," I said, glancing at the jumble of envelopes. "How was Anna at the pickup today?"

"Well, I heard some interesting things about our school," he said. "Kind of alarming, actually." He sat down at the computer and turned it on.

"Oh," I said, suddenly feeling a stab of irritation. "And just *who* did you hear these things from?"

"People . . ." he said vaguely.

"You mean like unhappily married ex-girlfriends?!"

"Oh, God, Laura, don't start with all that again!"

Out of the corner of my eye, I saw an image from the Iguana Cay brochure appear as the background on Richard's desktop screen—the three palm trees on a sandbar floating on a turquoise sea, with a sailboat off on the horizon. In the back of my mind, I wondered how on earth Richard had managed to find that photo and put it on his desktop. But for the moment, I was caught up in an argument spiraling out of control.

"I read her love notes on your e-mail!" I burst out. "I know all about you and Amy!"

"You read my e-mails!" He seemed genuinely shocked. "You've been snooping on me?"

"Yes! And I know about *Abelard*!"

"Huh?!"

"Your grocery store password!"

"Yeah?"

"And Amy's favorite philosopher!"

"You're clinical," he said. "I picked Abelard because the 'lard' reminded me of all the bacon and butter and stuff we were buying."

My chest clenched up. Dominique, Bronwyn, Richard—everybody had betrayed me.

"She said you are her one true love!" I sobbed.

"She did not! She used the past tense! She said I *was* once, long ago, in some imaginary past. . . ."

"Don't you see what she's trying to do? How can you be so blind?"

"Don't you see what you're doing? You're saying you don't trust me! You're spying on me, imagining all sorts of ridiculous plots. In fact, Amy—"

"Arghh! Don't say that woman's name!"

"Why are you so incapable of rational thought? It's like you can't see from A to B. You're so illogical, you can't even turn on a toaster without burning yourself!"

"A toaster? So now you don't like the way I toast bread? Let me tell you, buddy, you don't have a clue about people!"

"You're just like your brother," he said. "You think you're a victim, when the only person to blame for your problems is yourself!"

"How dare you bring James into this!" I cried. "I know where you got your mean streak! You're just like your father!"

We knew all of each other's hot buttons, and for the first time, neither of us hesitated to slam down on each one as viciously as we could. Our reading habits, our film preferences, our body shapes—suddenly, nothing was safe. I had never realized just how difficult it could be to share your life with someone. I had never known how many things he found wrong with me. And I discovered myself saying things about him I'd never said before, even to myself.

"If I'm so rotten, why did you marry me?" he yelled at last.

"I'm sorry I did!" I yelled back.

"I'm sorry, too!"

"Eeeeeeee!" Anna screamed, slicing through our fight. "Stop it! Stop it!" She began crying and hitting the sofa.

Once again, Anna's cries shocked me, bringing me back down to earth. Richard and I looked at her guiltily. We sat down on either side of her, trying to comfort her. But, as if by tacit agreement, we avoided touching each other.

"We're sorry," we both said.

"Daddy doesn't mean to shout," I said, clenching my teeth.

"And Mommy doesn't mean what she says," Richard said.

We glared at each other like a pair of samurai on the battle-field, too exhausted to go on fighting but trained never to give up.

"Say *please!*" Anna demanded. "Say *thank you!*"

Richard and I grimaced at each other and said the magic words. Anna was right: They calmed us down. I glanced somberly at my husband. How could things have gotten to this point? We sat in silence for a few moments.

I glanced at the pile of mail in front of me. All of a sudden, I noticed that one of the envelopes was on Metropolitan stationery. It had no postmark.

"Hey, where'd this come from?" I asked.

"Sunny's assistant gave this to me when I picked up Anna," Richard said. "She said it was for you. But *I* don't go around read-ing other people's mail."

I picked up the envelope and started to open it.

"So what did Amy tell you, anyway?" I asked, suddenly realiz-ing that I was quite curious.

"Amy said she discovered that her husband had to make a, uh, donation to Sunny in order to get Anna into—"

Before he could finish, the phone rang.

"*Allo?* Laura, is it really you?" It was Dominique.

To my astonishment, she seemed overjoyed to reach me. "I have been longing to tell you something," she said. Her voice was brimming with excitement. "I'm sorry we have not had a chance to speak. I have been so busy! So much has happened! We must talk!"

"Yes, we must talk!" I said impatiently. "But maybe not——"

"I have found a man who appreciates me!" she squealed into the phone. "A man of purpose!"

"Dominique!"

"Do not be alarmed, *cherie*! Be happy for me! I believe we are going to meet someplace far away, in another world, and then nothing will hold us back from our fate."

Richard looked at me impatiently, stomping his feet like a bull ready to resume the fight.

"Dominique, get a hold of yourself! This is real life, not some soap opera! Do you know what you're doing?"

"Eh? Yes, but you don't, do you? I mean, I haven't told you yet!" She said it as though I were an actor who had misread a cue.

"I'm sorry," I said. "We need to talk. But right now I'm in the middle of something important. I have to call you back. . . ."

As I tried to extricate myself from the conversation, my eye strayed once again to the computer image on Richard's desktop, the three palm trees on a sandbar with a sailboat hovering on turquoise water in the distance. I began to feel very unwell.

"He gives me the most fantastic presents, you know," Dominique was saying. "He is a man of such taste! Last week he gave me a *fantastique* handbag I had my eye on at Fendi! He knows me so well! It is like we have known each other forever!"

In a panic, I handed the envelope to Richard and motioned for him to open it.

"He tells me we must have been soul mates in another life," I distractedly heard Dominique saying, as Richard finished reading the letter. He got up from his chair, his mouth falling open.

"I will tell you more soon!" Dominique continued. "I am still so surprised myself!"

I hung up.

My heart felt like it had fallen into quicksand. We looked at each other.

Richard sat back down. "You'd better read the letter before you go on," he said, his voice weary.

Picking it up, I scanned the letter. By now I knew what it would say.

> We at the Metropolitan School feel most fortunate to have been able to share our lives and experiences with you and Anna. It is with great sadness that we now conclude we must continue our journeys along separate paths. It has come to our attention that Anna's developmental profile is more complex than we were initially led to believe. We do not feel that we possess the professional resources to adequately address her behavioral and developmental issues at this time. Anna's expulsion is effective immediately. In order to minimize possible trauma to other students, we require that you not appear within one hundred yards of the school for the remainder of the school year.
>
> With joy and hopes of healing,
> Sunny

Richard joined me on the bed, and we sat huddled together. I realized that he was genuinely shocked and really worried. Maybe he cared more about Anna's prestigious school than he liked to reveal.

"I don't get it," he kept saying. "What the hell happened?"

I shook my head. I was such a fool to have trusted Sunny. I blinked at the paper in front of me. Everything was crumbling into emptiness.

I had thrown away a perfectly good scholarship to the most desirable preschool in Manhattan. Perhaps there was something rotten at Metropolitan. Perhaps it was a snake pit. But so what? Most Manhattan mothers managed to play the game without getting their kids expelled. Not me. I had to stick my nose where it didn't belong. I had snooped, gossiped, slandered, and drawn a series of wrong conclusions. I had failed. My daughter would lose out on a decent preschool experience, and now I'd never turn in my professional assignments on time. How would I manage?

I stared glumly at the image on Richard's computer desktop. Three palm trees on a bar of sand. A grain of suspicion began to form in my mind.

"Where did you get that photo?" I asked.

"Our daughter has just been expelled from preschool and you want to know about my desktop background?" he asked, incredulous.

"Yes," I said firmly.

"It's from the sample desktop-photo file," he said, sounding annoyed. "It's one of a couple dozen photos that comes with every version of Windows. It's probably from some generic beach in the Bahamas."

We looked at each other in silence for several seconds. But my mind was whirring a million miles an hour. It was all clicking into place. All of a sudden, it was all mapped out before me as clear and bright as the Caribbean sunlight. I could see every one of my many missteps. I had been wrong about everything. But somehow, in my gut, I had been right all along.

"I need you to take care of Anna tomorrow," I said, my voice suddenly rising. "Call a car service. And where's my credit card? I've got to act. Now!"

Chapter 16

Rub a dub-dub
Three men in a tub
And who do you think they be?

The sun was hotter than it had been in my fantasies. The sky was more hazy than blue. Every now and then, the suggestion of a breeze wafted over the sea, and I turned my damp face toward it greedily. I sipped my virgin mimosa, the ice long since melted into an unhealthy-looking foam, and picked at my plate of jerk-fried eggs with mango sauce, compliments of the Sun & Frolic public-relations department. Around me were scattered the mostly empty plastic tables and chairs of the vast SeaView Terrace (seating capacity 850). Off in the distance, only a few outcroppings of rock interrupted the flat, blue-green horizon. Down by the dock, my new friend Victor waved to me from his small launch, and I waved back, giving the signal for him to keep waiting.

As I took in the Caribbean air—the *real* Caribbean air this time—I felt grounded at last. The illusions of the past weeks were gone. I no longer even regretted the many wrong turns that had brought me to this point. I looked back on what I had thought and felt and how I had behaved in the recent past as a kind of curiosity, a test case of what could happen to an ordinary mother under extraordinary conditions. Now I was ready for action.

Dominique at last descended for brunch. She was in a flowing white dress that had more holes than fabric. She looked like a deconstructed sailboat as she made her way toward me across the sea of empty tables.

"It is very gauche, this Sun and Frolic place, no?" she said, looking askance at the vast expanse of plastic on the terrace. "I really cannot wait to leave and go to Iguana Cay!"

I smiled thinly behind my sunglasses. It had been so easy to persuade Dominique to come down to Sun & Frolic on the Turks and Caicos. I told her that there was going to be an interisland meeting on Iguana Cay, and that I had been invited to attend on behalf of my client. I mentioned—as though it were of no particular concern—that Jeffrey would attend in his capacity as Iguana-in-chief.

In fact, I had simply blustered my way to a free room with the PR department of Sun & Frolic, which hardly had a shortage of rooms, and booked the flight on the corporate charge card, figuring that by the time Carter found out he'd have already decided to fire me anyway.

Dominique had immediately bought herself a first-class plane ticket. She had arrived in the Providenciales airport as though she was on a honeymoon. I spotted her leading a trail of porters who struggled with her overstuffed suitcases and hatboxes. By the time she had finished checking in, it was past midnight. Although I knew she was as eager to have a private talk as I was, albeit not the same one, we had not yet had enough time alone to really get started.

"I sometimes feel that the universe is so full," she now said, waving away the waiter, who was plying pseudo-Caribbean brunch specialties.

The prologue having been spoken, she placed a crocodile handbag, with a chrome clasp of interlocking F's, over the back of her chair.

"It is from my lover," she announced, following my eyes. The curtain had gone up.

I feigned surprise. "Who would that be?"

"I cannot say," she announced with a flourish. "Even I am surprised. I had thought love would find me from the bottom, from the gutters in the streets, but I have found it in a palace. Who would have guessed? Perhaps I am not Miss Julie after all."

This was more disturbing than I had expected it to be. Dominique's head was in the clouds at the best of times, but her heart was in the right place, and she was my friend. Now she seemed only vaguely aware that she was torpedoing her marriage, not only desecrating her life and Alan's but devastating their daughter's as well.

When she came back to earth, would she really be glad she had left her husband and embarked on a new life with Jeffrey in his "palace"? I seriously doubted it. She would remain interested in Jeffrey only as long as he could maintain himself as some undefined endpoint of her feverish fantasies. For Dominique, more than for most people, the sense of anticipation was everything—

I realized that without the uneasiness that impelled her forward, her existence lacked any direction at all.

Sitting across from her on the SeaView Terrace, I didn't have the courage to pick up the sledgehammer of reality and shatter her illusions just yet. For all her shortcomings, there was still a way in which I admired her. I was too quick to leap to dire conclusions on the slightest pretext, and it had all but wrecked my marriage and my life. Dominique was heading in the same direction. But at least she wasn't prepared to abandon her sense of life's unbounded possibilities.

"So let us go to the island," she said, her voice shimmering with undisguised longing.

"We will," I promised. "We just have to wait for, uh . . . Kim!"

Off on the other side of the SeaView Terrace, I spotted Kim. She was marching over to our table, wearing an intimidating khaki outfit that made her look like a Special Operations officer setting out on a hunt for terrorist ducks. I breathed a sigh of relief. While she had been incommunicado in Texas with her bloodthirsty investors, I had only been able to leave a string of frantic messages on her voicemail. In a desperate effort to ensure that she would come, I had warned her that Bronwyn was maneuvering to claim the best Royal Villa and blackball her own application in the process. The only way to stop Bronwyn, I said, was to come down and claim dibs.

"Kim?" Dominique whispered to me, looking hurt. "I mean, she is a fine woman, but why is she here?"

"She's buying a Royal Villa, too," I pointed out a little defensively. "I couldn't leave her behind. She'll help us, you'll see."

"It is okay." Dominique shrugged, clearly disappointed that the tales of her secret love life were temporarily put on hold. "As long as she does not talk about who killed that stupid rat!"

Kim greeted Dominique with eyebrows raised high in surprise but evidently decided to act casual.

"You wouldn't believe how many ducks died in Texas this weekend," she said, shaking her head and settling into her seat. She picked up a menu. "What have they got that's vegetarian?"

After placing an order for pineapple kebab salad from the waiter, she turned to me. "So, what's the rush? How come you didn't give me time to change?"

"Well, we're scheduled to leave for Iguana Cay in a few minutes," I said evasively.

Kim looked at Dominique.

"I assume she's coming, too?"

"Well," I stammered. "We may actually be four . . . Bronwyn! Hello!"

Bronwyn was approaching our table, stiff as a Popsicle in her perfect pink summer suit. She was wearing a large, floppy straw hat with a matching pink bow. Kim almost fell over in her seat. Of course, I'd had to tell Bronwyn pretty much the same story I told Kim—that I had discovered her dreaded rival was planning to claim the best Villa on Iguana Cay and blackball her. The trickiest part was just getting the message to Bronwyn, since she had blocked all my calls. So I finally wrote her a brief letter and sent it over via messenger using an old envelope from Metropolitan—something I was sure she would open.

"I thought I might find you here," Bronwyn said tersely.

"I couldn't let you have all the fun," Kim snapped.

"This better be good." Bronwyn glowered at me.

"I've lost my appetite." Kim slammed down her napkin. "Let's go already!"

I waved frantically to Victor. It seemed like a good idea to get on the move before Kim and Bronwyn came to blows.

We walked down to the boat launch in silence. The sun was starting to burn off the morning haze, and the air was bright and clear. Beneath the weather-beaten dock, a school of small fish were swimming parallel to the beach, their silvery scales flashing.

"Everybody ready?" Victor said as he helped us onto the bobbing vessel. I grinned nervously at him while the others just glared quietly.

We took seats facing each other on the benches lining the back of the boat. Victor started up the feeble motor, and the boat slowly pulled out to sea. The light breeze felt good on my skin. I put my arm over the side and trailed my finger in the water as we moved along, watching the wake form behind it.

The boat gently skimmed across the turquoise waves. I looked at the sunlight playing on the glittery surface of the ocean. Suddenly, it reminded me of the colors on Sunny's opal, glistening in the sunlight that streamed into the classrooms at Metropolitan. I started to feel seasick.

Bronwyn had her hand on her hat to keep it from flying away, and I saw that she, too, looked as though she was getting queasy. She was still furious. When we were well out to sea, she turned to Kim and asked, "How's your poor kid?"

Kim wrinkled her face in disgust. "Save it, sister," she said. "I know who iced Snowflake, and I know why!"

Bronwyn looked at her with disbelief.

"*That* is just *ridiculous!*" she said. "*My* son didn't kill that hamster."

"*And* I also know why you bought a Royal Villa!" Kim said.

"I know why *you* bought one! *Everybody* knows about Jake!"

"Hey!" I said, trying to stop the collision.

"What I can't figure out is why you are stealing from the auction budget," Kim interrupted me, shouting at Bronwyn. "Maybe you need the extra money to pay for Harrison's therapy." In the mad rush of the past couple days, I hadn't yet told Kim that Bronwyn had nothing to do with the purloined Fendi.

"No!" I interjected. "Dominique has the handbag."

I pointed to the bag, which Dominique was holding on her lap.

Dominique lifted it up. "I love it," she said, admiring the elegant crocodile skin.

"But you bought that with school money!" Kim said.

"I did not buy this!" Dominique protested.

Bronwyn's eyes popped open. "Oh my God," she said. "Of course it was Emmy! She killed Snowflake! It's always the one you'd least expect!"

"Hey!" I said. "That's not what I meant!"

"Do not be so silly!" Dominique interrupted. "Emmy is a girl!" She looked at me in disgust. "I knew we would end up talking about that stupid rat! Besides, it is Laura's daughter who has been expelled! It is because Laura lied to the school about her problems!"

Bronwyn and Kim looked at me in shock.

"Expelled? Anna's been expelled? Is it true?" they asked simultaneously.

"Yes, but I can explain. . . ."

"You dragged us down here and your daughter isn't even at Metropolitan anymore?" Bronwyn said, incredulous. "Did Anna kill Snowflake?"

"Zip it, Bronwyn," Kim said, rising to my defense. "We all know Harrison goes to a shrink."

"I . . . Harrison does *not* go to a shrink!"

"Then just who is Dr. Dan?" Kim fired back, ignoring my efforts to quiet them down.

"Dan is not . . ." Bronwyn seemed to be choking. Then she put on a fierce look. "*You're* the one who carts your kid off to Bellevue!"

Kim's mouth dropped open. Her eyes reddened.

"I am not taking him to Bellevue!" she shrieked, suddenly losing her composure. "You're the one with a Web browser full of sadomasochistic *porn!*"

Bronwyn reeled like she had been slapped in the face. "How do you know what's on my computer?"

She looked away from us, her mouth slack and her eyes filled with confusion. All of a sudden, she lowered her head and started to cry. Kim looked unsure of herself, wondering what she had done.

"Hey," I said softly, putting my arm around Bronwyn. She shook me off.

"Why did you bring me here? Why do I have to see that horrible woman?" she sobbed.

"She's not who you think she is," I said to Bronwyn. I looked searchingly at Kim and decided to take the risk. "Kim, why don't you tell Bronwyn why you bring Jake to Bellevue?"

Kim looked at me dumbly. I could see her eyes begin to narrow, the accusation of betrayal forming in her mind.

"Kim, you have to trust me!" I pleaded. "Bronwyn isn't who you think she is, either! I learned so much while you were gone. Please!"

Kim just sat there, staring at us.

"Maybe Bronwyn will tell you about Dr. Dan," I said. "Look! We're all in the same boat!" I winced at my own corniness but held fast.

For a few moments we all stayed silent, hearing only the gentle hum of the motor and the water slapping against the sides of the vessel. Bronwyn heaved a great sob. Kim wore a quizzical expression on her face, just as she had when I'd caught up with her at the hospital.

She began to speak slowly. "Bronwyn, I . . . I'm sorry. Maybe there's been a misunderstanding. You see, Eric, my husband, he is a good father and he means well. . . ."

Bronwyn listened raptly as Kim told her the story of Eric's battle with drug addiction. When Kim talked about Eric, I could see only James. I gazed out at the wide sea, the rich world of its depths forever hidden from view, and thought how much I wished my brother were with me now.

When Kim finished, she eyed Bronwyn suspiciously, as though steeling herself for another attack. But Kim didn't know Bronwyn as I did.

Bronwyn melted like strawberry ice cream in the hot summer sun. She put her hat in her lap and reached over to touch Kim. "I'm so sorry I said anything about Jake. I really misread the whole situation," she said through her tears. "You know, in a way you're lucky," she whispered. "It sounds like Eric is really struggling to get his life together again. It can't be easy for him, fighting an addiction like that. It proves just how much he loves you and Jake."

She paused. "I only wish Lloyd would try . . ."

She stopped. I held her hand. She looked around quietly. Then, with the Caribbean breeze blowing lightly through her hair, she told us about Lloyd.

When Lloyd and Bronwyn had first met at the bank, they tried to keep their affair private. Weekends together were passionate and clandestine. But as soon as they publicly announced their relationship—and their intention to marry—Lloyd's ardor cooled. Bronwyn thought he was anxious about the wedding. She figured it would pass. It only got worse.

Lloyd barely touched Bronwyn when she was pregnant. His trips out of town were longer and more frequent. Soon after Harrison's birth, Bronwyn started to track Lloyd's credit-card receipts. He'd say he was in Mexico City when really he was in Rio. She confronted him. He said it was all a misunderstanding, and the strange credit-card activity stopped. But Lloyd's behavior became more and more erratic. One night, when he was supposedly in Tokyo, a friend of Bronwyn's bumped into him in a midtown bar. He was with a young woman with fake hair and fake breasts and a Russian accent. Bronwyn confronted him again, and he pleaded for another chance. But it was all a lie.

Finally, Bronwyn gave him an ultimatum: couples therapy or divorce. Lloyd refused therapy, so she ended up seeing Dr. Dan on her own.

"I just don't think it's going to work," she said, weeping. "But I'm too scared to leave. I don't know how I'd manage with the kids. What can I do?"

"My God," Dominique said. "If he is making you so unhappy, you must do *something!*"

Bronwyn began to cry uncontrollably. "But what can I do? My first marriage was a failure, and now this. There must be something wrong with me. My mom still thinks Lloyd is Prince Charming. What about Harrison and Tess? The school will never accept . . ."

"I'm so sorry." Kim put her arm around Bronwyn. "Please don't blame yourself," she said tenderly. "It's not your fault." A cool breeze came up from the ocean.

After Bronwyn had quieted down, Kim suddenly shot Dominique a puzzled look. "So, how'd you get that expensive bag? Who gave it to you?"

"I am sworn not to say!" Dominique gathered herself up dramatically. "He made me swear on my life. My *life!*"

"Dominique," I chided her. "You'd better tell."

"No! It is about love! You know nothing about love! It must never be spoken!"

"Anyway, what do you know about love?" Kim asked peevishly. "We're not in high school anymore. We're married mothers now. Real love is about perseverance, and commitment, and getting through the bad times and the good. It's not some silly fantasy. *You* need to grow up."

"What do you know of fantasy?" Dominique said contemptuously. "Fantasy is like a fine champagne. Of course, I mean, *you* could drink water from the kitchen sink all of your life . . ."

"I know who gave you the bag," said Bronwyn cattily. "You did, because you're in love with yourself!"

Dominique turned her head and looked out at the ocean.

"You had better tell them, Dominique," I said. "Or I will."

"Very well, then," Dominique said histrionically. "I see I have no choice. My secret admirer is . . . Jeffrey Forsythe!"

Bronwyn and Kim started with surprise. Bronwyn screwed up her face with disgust. But I saw a look of alarm spread across Kim's face.

"So Jeffrey stole the money for the bag from the auction committee. . . ." Kim started to say.

"Actually, I think Sunny may have done the legwork for him," I said. "But now, Dominique, would you please say who told you to tell Bronwyn that Kim had already bought a membership in the Iguana Club?"

"It was Jeffrey, of course!" Dominique said. "When we first spoke to each other properly, as man and woman, in the Hotel Gansevoort."

"You mean Kim didn't buy a membership before me?" Bronwyn asked, confused.

"No! I told you, I only bought one because you bought one!" Kim said, looking worried.

"But I only bought one because you bought one. . . ."

"But . . ."

"Ladies, you will want to remove your shoes." Victor's deep voice suddenly cut through our thoughts.

The boat came to a stop with a gravelly, scraping sound on the bottom. We had pulled up to a rocky beach. Victor jumped out and heaved the boat higher onto the sand. He reached for our hands, one by one, and helped us out of the vessel. We landed in ankle-deep water and waded through the shallow waves and up to the beach.

"I don't get it," Bronwyn said, oblivious to the change in scene. "So who killed Snowflake?"

Victor led us to a shady thicket of coconut palms, where we discovered a narrow dirt path. Pausing to put our shoes back on, we followed it up a small incline. As we reached the top, we found ourselves standing on an islet of barren red rocks that was about the size of one of the old industrial buildings in TriBeCa, surrounded on all sides by the azure waters of the Caribbean. There were almost no trees, just tiny shrubs sticking up from the crevices. Bird droppings covered the rocks everywhere we looked.

"What are we doing here?" Kim said nervously.

Dominique scanned the horizon, her hair blowing about in the wind. "But where is Iguana Cay?" she asked Victor.

Victor just smiled and spread his arms.

Suddenly, we heard a rustling sound. A leathery lizard the size of small alligator pulled out from behind a rock and chased another, smaller one away. Across the islet, dozens of lizards of various sizes sunned themselves on the red rocks. Some were about the size of my thumb. Others were two, three, or more feet in length, with arched backs, serrated fins on top, and long tails. Every now and then they'd move about, looking for food or shooing each other off the most desirable perches.

"The iguanas love it here," said Victor, still beaming. "This is their heaven."

I pointed to the small sign that had been placed on one of the rocks. In chipped, sun-beaten paint, it read: "Welcome to Iguana Cay. Please respect our wildlife!"

Kim's mouth dropped open. "Holy fuck!" she whispered. "We've been scammed!"

Dominique gasped. "He has lied to me!"

Bronwyn turned to me. "So if it wasn't any of the kids . . ." I could see the thoughts churning behind her honey-colored eyes. "She really knew how to play us," she finally said with a faraway, almost ethereal expression. "It was Sunny who killed Snowflake, wasn't it?"

Chapter 17

There was a crooked man
Who walked a crooked mile

It was just past midnight when Kim pried open the bathroom window. Dominique and I clambered in.

In the dim glow of Dominique's flashlight, I could see Kim brushing little cotton balls off her black jeans and sweater. "The closet was filthy," she complained in a whisper. "We had to hide in the art room."

"My God, this toilet is so *little*," Dominique said, flashing the beam at the potty.

Kim looked at her oddly. "It's for children."

"Where's Bronwyn?" I hissed urgently.

"Follow me," Kim said, leading us to Sunny's office with her own flashlight.

Bronwyn was seated at Sunny's desk, flipping through a stack of folders under a desk lamp. A couple of cotton balls stuck to her hair and gray cashmere cardigan. Her nose was pink and peeling from our day in the Caribbean sun.

That day, after our revelatory visit to Iguana Cay, we had returned to my hotel room at Sun & Frolic to make sense of our findings. For the first time since the school year began, we were operating as a true team. That night, Bronwyn and Kim's rivalry was set aside as they discovered each other as friends. With all the persuasiveness we had at our disposal, we questioned Dominique about her situation with Jeffrey, urging her to realize that she, too, had been duped.

Now, back in New York, we had sneaked into Metropolitan late at night, determined to figure out the missing pieces of the puzzle.

"It's hard to make sense of all this," Bronwyn said, waving with exasperation at the stack of papers. "Kim, you've gotta help me here!"

It made me smile involuntarily to hear her speaking to Kim as a friend rather than a competitor. Kim pulled up a chair and sat next to her.

I crammed in next to them and poked at a key on Sunny's computer. It immediately came to life——she had obviously left it in sleep mode. I rummaged through her desktop, not quite sure what I was looking for. I clicked on a file called "IC Presentation" and found a folder with the familiar slide show on Iguana Cay. I flicked it on, and Dominique threw herself onto the L-shaped sofa across from the desk with a great sigh.

"You alright?" I asked.

"I have been such a fool," she announced.

"At least now you know the truth." Kim nodded soberly.

"I wish I never met that man with every fiber of my being," Dominique wailed.

"Tell us precisely what you said to Alan," Bronwyn ordered. "I want to hear the exact words." Dominique had already related the story of how, just after purchasing her plane ticket, she had told Alan that she felt as though she were suffocating, and said she "needed to be free." But she hadn't exactly confessed her affair to him, and Bronwyn wasn't sure he'd figured it out.

"Do you think there's a chance he doesn't know about you and Jeffrey?" Bronwyn asked. "I mean, maybe if he doesn't know the details . . ."

"The details do not matter," Dominique said forcefully. "In his heart, Alan knows everything. He is not a fool, my Alan. Not like me. And he is suffering so much. I did not imagine how he would suffer." She looked at the floor.

"When I came in from the airport today, I found his note. He is staying with friends. And he has taken Emmy." Her voice shook, and for the first time since I'd known her, her fragility seemed genuine.

She added, "I am really ashamed of what I have done."

"You know that's illegal," Kim said from her position at the desk. "He can't remove Emmy from her primary residence without a court ruling. Do you want to call the police?"

"I do not want the police," Dominique said simply. "I want my family to come back."

While Dominique wrung her hands, I looked into the folder where the images for the slide show were stored. Presumably,

Sunny and Jeffrey were planning to run the slide show during the auction. I opened the file properties and examined them for clues. All of a sudden, I noticed the tiny print on the border of one of the images.

"Check this out," I squealed, pointing to an especially appealing Iguana Cay beach scene. "This photo is courtesy of the Kona Village Resort on the Big Island of Hawaii!"

I flipped through several others.

"Oh my gosh!" I said as I examined them.

The other photos, I discovered, came from a variety of archives from places as far afield as the Maldives, Australia, and Bora-Bora. With a quick Internet search, I found most of the originals on readily accessible websites. Here, free to everyone, were all the bits and pieces of the familiar images that had gone into making up the mythical island of Iguana Cay. The houses draped in bougainvillea, the endless white-sand beaches, the lush gardens blooming with bird-of-paradise and ginger lilies, infinity-edge plunge pools, the luxury bathtubs, the bowls of fresh-picked tropical fruit, and all the rest. Jeffrey had cropped, shopped, and mixed the photos, fitting a beautiful villa from one shot onto a beach from another, adding a few extra hues to a sunset here, brushing out an unnecessary cloud there to invent a mythical paradise in the Turks and Caicos. His only mistake was to have used the generic three-palm-trees-on-a-sandbar shot, possibly not realizing that it was not only on some remote website but also a regular part of Windows software.

"This is great!" Bronwyn said. "We need to collect as much evidence as possible!"

As I flicked through the photos, I began to appreciate Jeffrey's talent. From the thousands of available images, he had chosen just the right ones to illustrate an irresistible story about a unique tropical utopia.

"I wish I could turn Sun and Frolic into a place like Iguana Cay!" I said to no one in particular.

Kim looked up from her papers. "Why don't you?" she said sharply, with a certain glint in her eye. I looked at her in surprise. I knew I wouldn't take her up on this wild suggestion. But for someone like Kim, such a bold move was a logical step. I suddenly understood why she was such a success in business. It wasn't because she was the smartest person in the room; it was because she had the courage to dream big. Her own improbable journey from postwar Korea to small-town Utah to the world of Manhattan high finance had given her an unshakable faith in people's abilities to forge their own destinies.

"Wow," Kim said, poring over sheets of numbers she had pulled from Sunny's desk. "There are some major-income items here. But I don't understand where the money is coming from. There's one hundred thousand dollars attributed to 'carrot,' and the same again for 'nino' and 'blondie.' "

"Oh my God, Kim, don't you see?" Bronwyn blurted out. "Nino is Emilio and Pilar's kid! This was bribe money to get the kids into the school!"

Carrot, we figured out, was Pearl Necklace's little brat, and blondie was Amy and Wesley's spawn, the other Anna.

"You're kidding," I heard Bronwyn whisper to Kim.

"No, just look," Kim said, waving some papers in front of us.

Dominique and I turned to her. "Sunny's figured out what a Metropolitan education is really worth to these parents."

"So she's cashing in big-time!" Bronwyn said.

"Or at least she thinks she is," Kim said, her eyes scanning the papers spread out in front of her. She pulled some papers out from her briefcase and frowned as she compared the numbers. "My guess is she doesn't know the difference between an LLC and a PLC."

I had no idea what the difference was; either. But I could tell that Kim was seeing something unexpected in the files.

"My God, Kim, please speak English, I do not understand you," Dominique yelled from her prone position on the couch. "What is a TLC?"

"Never mind all that," Kim replied. "The gist of it is that all the money Sunny's been raising has gone into a black hole . . ."

She shuffled through some more papers. "Actually, not quite a black hole." Her voice grew steely. She held up a bank statement. "The money has been transferred to the Iguana Cay Holding Company."

"But Iguana Cay does not even exist!" Dominique cried.

"Only on the name of a bank account in Switzerland," Kim said. "But they've set it up so that it looks like the money is funneled back through me before it disappears. And they forged my signature on title deeds. So I'm supposedly vouching for the properties. I'm supposed to take the fall!"

"No!" We were livid.

Kim continued grimly, "This isn't some rinky-dink plan. I bet they plotted this out a long time ago. They used me! I bet they found out my husband's in rehab. Who's gonna believe the wife of a drug addict? The bastards!"

"Is Sunny in on it?" Bronwyn asked incredulously.

"No," Kim replied. "Even she's been had."

Together we reexamined Sunny's story in light of this new information. She had watched as her neighborhood was overrun with über-gentry, and had accepted their children gladly into her school. After receiving so much fawning attention from the rich and famous, she began to fancy that she was one of them. Only she didn't have the money to pay for all the designer clothes, spa vacations, and summers in the Hamptons that she needed in order to really feel like their equal.

"It is *classique*," said Dominique sadly. "A governess, basically, who cannot stand to be a governess. She wants to be the grande dame. In France, you know, if the girl is young, she will try to steal your husband." She shrugged. "But not if she is older, like Sunny."

So Sunny turned the school into a personal moneymaking machine. Then Jeffrey figured out her game.

"It takes a con to know a con," Bronwyn said grimly. I could see that she was still struggling with the reality of her situation with Lloyd.

"Only Sunny didn't realize that Jeffrey was planning to con her, too," Kim added. "His plan is to use her to raise all the money from the school body for Iguana Cay, then make off with it himself."

"And we helped him do it," Bronwyn said. "Sunny played us against each other perfectly. Killing Snowflake was genius. She knew we'd be so busy trying to use it to knock each other out of Holyfield, we wouldn't concentrate on the auction."

Dominique, who had sat up on the sofa and was disconsolately twirling her crimson scarf, suddenly spoke up. "His name is not Jeffrey, by the way."

We looked at her intently.

"I heard Eve talk to him on the phone. She was angry with him, speaking too loud. I heard her voice. 'Now you listen to me, Ted Kelly,' she said." Dominique wrinkled her nose. "I have to say she sounded very weird. Like an angry *laundresse*."

We paused to digest. "Didn't it bother you that your lover was using an alias?" Kim asked, a little impatient.

"I . . . I thought perhaps he was a secret agent," Dominique said ruefully. "It seemed so romantic."

"You already have a romantic male lead in your life," Bronwyn said. "His name is Alan."

"I know," Dominique said quietly.

Kim sat next to me at the computer and we began to conduct a Web search on Australian men named Ted Kelly. It took some time to wade through the false leads—the owner of a gas station in Sydney, an anesthesiologist in Brisbane, the president of a bank in Canberra, a soap-opera character—but we finally found our man. In an old issue of the *Queensland Times,* we saw a smiling photograph of the younger Jeffrey. Ted Kelly, it turned out, was descended from one of the infamous Australian outlaw Ned Kelly's meaner sisters. And he seemed intent on following in his famous ancestor's footsteps.

We tracked Ted Kelly's story through old online newspaper

clippings and sheriff's office reports. Seven years earlier, he had been at the center of a minor scandal among the well-to-do of Australia's Gold Coast. He had collected large amounts of money from wealthy families for investment in diamond mines in West Africa. But when some investors discovered that the mines were about the size of foxholes, Ted disappeared. Rumor had it he'd ended up in South Africa, but nobody knew for sure. Because so many important Australians were caught up in the scam, the government had been pressured into letting the matter drop in order to avoid embarrassment all around.

"So he probably spent all his money and figured he'd run a scam on us," I said.

"Yeah," Kim said. "He's going to raise a truckload of money from the rich and the stupid. Then, when people realize they've been conned, they'll be too embarrassed to pursue it, and he'll move on."

"He wants to move to Hollywood," Dominique announced glumly. "He plans to start a new career producing films. He has promised he will make a film starring—"

"We've got to stop him!" Bronwyn said. "We've got less than forty-eight hours before the auction!"

"We need to call the police," Kim said.

"Of course, you realize that if we expose Jeffrey, the school will suffer, too," I said, thinking aloud.

We sat silently around the desk lamp in the dark room.

"I guess we don't have a choice," Bronwyn said, faltering. "I'll find a new place for Harrison and Tess. They're all I have. . . ."

Kim and Dominique, too, looked subdued. We knew now that

the school was rotten to the core. But it had marked what we all felt was one of the great successes in our lives as mothers. We had all assumed the grand status of Metropolitan moms, and it was difficult to reconcile ourselves to the reality that we would have to start the Manhattan preschool dance basically from scratch.

"We'll be looking for a place midyear, halfway through pre-K, and coming from a school with a pretty awful record," Bronwyn said bitterly.

"I suppose I could send Emmy to the *Lycee Francaise,*" said Dominique. "If Alan ever lets me see her again."

"And I bet all the other schools are just as corrupt," Kim said. "God, I wish we could just have the damn school we thought we were applying for, not this mess."

I looked at her intently. I remembered the advice she'd given me about Sun & Frolic.

"Well, why can't we?" I said boldly. The other women looked at me, startled. An audacious plan was starting to form in my mind.

"Why can't we?" I repeated, looking each one squarely in the face. "Why can't we take back our school?"

Chapter 18

Rich man, poor man
Beggar man, thief

"Children's table-and-chairs set, hand-painted in organic pigments by Miss Caspar's four-year-olds class . . ."

With the help of a microphone, Sunny's booming voice filled the raucous cavern of Greenbacks, a restaurant situated in a former bank in lower TriBeCa. It echoed off the massive marble columns and the domed ceiling with its fading nineteenth-century vision of utopia; skipped along the ornate crenellations, brass handrails, and the wooden teller counters that now served as a bar; and landed with a splash at the giant, artificial tropical island in the center of the room, a pile of powder-white sand planted with a grove of fake palm trees surrounded by a foot of water.

Everywhere, soused Metropolitan parents sat around the island at dozens of large tables, wearing the straw hats and Brazilian flip-flops that were handed out at the door, picking at platters of grilled lobster tails and marinated conch, and slugging down tall glasses of perfectly mixed mojitos. A troupe of brightly dressed dancers moved around the floor entertaining clusters of tables, and a steel drum trio filled in gaps in the program with calypso tunes.

"Do I hear one thousand dollars?" Sunny said, her voice bursting with enthusiasm. She was wearing a purple skirt and matching three-quarter-sleeve jacket. From her neck dangled her trademark opal. Now it was keeping company with another pendant—a sparkling golden stone that looked to be almost as big as Eve's yellow sapphire.

The parents, loud with rum, drove the bidding up to $5,000 for a table and chairs that probably didn't break $200 at Home Depot, including the organic paints.

When no one was looking, I carefully readjusted the sock stuffed into the front of my pants, which had slipped into a very compromising position. I tried to relieve my breasts from their agony by pulling through my shirt at my sadistically tight sports bra. I made a note to myself: Next time I cross-dress, I'm going for a baggier look.

My transformation from woman into drag king had been Dominique's idea. "Sunny would never allow you into the auction as *Laura,*" she said. "You need to make a *real* disguise. You will be a waitress. *Mais non!* A waiter! A male waiter!" She knew just the place, she said, which turned out to be an apartment in the East Village with a sign above the door that read: Duke's Boot Camp for Girls Who Want to Be Boys.

When Dominique and I showed up for my appointment, "Duke" herself, a lanky redhead in a cowboy hat, engineer boots, and a Harley-Davidson T-shirt, looked me up and down, silently assessing my drag potential. She then bound my breasts, adjusted my jockstrap, picked out my clothes, affixed a pencil mustache to my upper lip with spirit gum, and spent hours instructing me on how to walk, sit, and otherwise impersonate an underemployed thespian named Laurance.

Agent Forte, who had been assigned to work with us by the local FBI, caught me fiddling with my sock from across the room and shot me a disapproving look. She could have given Duke a few tips; in her low-slung trousers, button-down shirt, and boxy jacket, she swaggered like a pro. Her short, black hair was slicked back with grease. I was starting to think she was awfully cute.

We'd had a mixed experience in our day of contact with the Feds. At first they were convinced that Kim and I were a couple of conspiracy nuts. Fortunately, we got through to a prosecutor named Agent Maxwell who had actually been following "Jeffrey's" exploits from a distance. "Ted Kelly?" he said. "He's a slippery one. Would've liked to have tailed him. But we haven't got the resources."

He also explained that so far there hadn't been much of a crime committed. "The money is being solicited for the school as a donation, right? So technically it's not an investment. If it's a fraud, we're better off waiting until they consummate the transaction. Otherwise, we don't have the authority to make arrests."

"Exactly," I told him. "That's why we want the auction to go ahead!" Maxwell seemed skeptical, but he said he'd send in Forte to help. Now I looked over at Forte and she hoisted a conspiratorial eyebrow.

Sunny put her hand on the microphone and leaned over, pendants clanking, to consult with Bronwyn, who was seated next to her at the head table. Bronwyn was dressed in fabulous South Seas pearls and a tiered broom skirt in keeping with the island theme, and she was doing a marvelous job of presiding over the auction with the aplomb of a society matron hosting a grand charity ball. I caught her eye and winked, and she beamed like the proud chairwoman of the auction committee that she was. Flanking Sunny on the other side were the two other members of the committee, Kim and Dominique. Kim was in a business suit, as always. Dominique was wearing her sea-green mermaid dress, her hair in an elaborate updo. She radiated screen-star glamour.

"Next item!" Sunny announced, taking a slip of paper from Bronwyn. "A pair of season tickets to the Knicks at Madison Square Garden . . . courtside seats!'

While the parents went into a bidding frenzy over the tickets, Amy, wearing a flowered dress that looked as though it was made out of sofa upholstery, beckoned me to her table. I caught my breath, but clearly neither she nor her husband next to her had any idea who I was. She demanded a glass of merlot. She didn't bother to look at me as I poured the wine. Then she glanced at her glass and loudly complained that it wasn't full. I filled it to the brim—one little steel-drum-trio vibration, and it was sure to spill—and walked away.

"Sixty-four thousand dollars!" Sunny brought down her gavel.

"Sold to Bill and Karen Seggermeyer!" She looked up. "That's India and Saffron's parents."

I caught a look of disbelief on Agent Forte's face across the room.

After checking with Bronwyn again, Sunny put up for bid the walk-on role in *Sex and the City: The Movie*. Kim made a few taps on the laptop discreetly placed at her side. The lights dimmed slightly and the super-sized plasma screen behind the head table flickered to life with the image of Sarah Jessica Parker.

"Oooh," Sarah cooed into the camera. "I just *love* Metro moms . . . and *dads*! You are all so . . . delicious!" She held up a Cosmopolitan and blew a kiss to us all.

Up at the front table, in a guayabera dress shirt and linen trousers, Emilio raised his paddle.

"Ten thousand dollars!" he announced.

He smiled with satisfaction at Pilar, who rolled her eyes in feigned chagrin. Next to them sat Eve, ethereal and expensive-looking in sleek silver silk, and the man known as Jeffrey.

Other parents joined in the bidding, but Emilio stood his ground, eventually claiming his role in *Sex and the City: The Movie* for $29,500.

"And now, the moment you've all been waiting for . . ." Sunny announced into the microphone.

New Age pipe sounds started to tinkle from the loudspeakers. The screen behind Sunny began to flash the all-too-familiar images. "Iguana Cay, more than a dream . . ." the soft, vaguely transatlantic voice intoned. I suddenly had a startling realization: It was Eve, talking with a pebble or two in her mouth.

As the voice trailed off into background music, Sunny briefly explained the terms of the Iguana Club auction. She needn't have bothered. In the week before the auction, the parent body of Metropolitan had convulsed with a frenzy of anticipation. Many, such as Bronwyn, Kim, and Dominique, had sent their money in ahead of time. Demand was so great, Sunny advised, that preference would be given to those new bidders who could make their deposits on the spot.

While Sunny spoke, the room filled up, with people lining the walls. Some were late-arriving parents, intent on catching the most important part of the auction. Others were parents at other preschools from around the city. Word had gotten around that this was the auction that counted. Everyone could see the value of the Iguana Club—it was going to include almost the entire board of Holyfield Academy.

The bidding for the first Deluxe Bungalow began at $100,000. It was one of the more modest units, far from the beach. Slipper Flats's husband immediately placed an offer. Pearl Necklace took it up a notch. Another pair joined in the fray. Parents began shouting encouragement. The room filled with the raucous sounds of chanting parents; it shook like a high-school gym during a pep rally. A red-faced man, well into his second bottle of wine, jumped in at $200,000. With the atmosphere at its electric peak, Slipper Flats took it to $210,000.

"Is that the final bid?" Sunny asked, looking around.

"It's the most we can do!" Slipper Flats squeaked, clasping her hands together pleadingly.

Sunny awarded the unit to Slipper Flats, and she took a bow to tremendous applause. "Of course, we will need a deposit," Sunny said in her cheerful schoolmarm voice.

Slipper Flats held up a piece of paper. It was a money order.

"Our deposit!" she announced giddily.

Sunny directed her to Jeffrey's assistant, Bruce, who had moved to the front table and was sitting in front of a large black box. While Sunny began describing the next luxury villa on the block, he took the deposit with a flourish and wrote a receipt for it.

With the crowd now primed to spend, the bidding for the next properties went even higher. Soon Metropolitan parents were shouting across the room at one another, trying to elbow each other out of the bidding, practically flinging their checks and money orders into the black box.

Emilio, twitching with impatience, saved the biggest bid of the night for an Imperial Estate. When he won it for a whopping $845,000, he picked up Pilar and gave her a big, wet kiss, which she tried unsuccessfully to deflect from her inflated lips. Then he put her down and ostentatiously waved Jeffrey's assistant over to collect a check.

At last, Sunny turned the podium over to Bronwyn to begin the wrap-up.

I glanced at Agent Forte. She made a funny gesture with her hand that looked like she was holding a garden hose. That, I assumed, was the signal.

I passed on the signal to Kim, who exchanged nods with Bronwyn and Dominique. I moved into position near the door.

"Ladies and gentlemen, parents of Metropolitan, we have an

announcement to make," Bronwyn said, standing up at the front table. Her voice wavered a bit, but she bravely faced the group.

That was supposed to be the cue for Agent Forte to move in. The plan was simple: We'd nab "Jeffrey" and Sunny right there, then explain to the parents that their donations to the auction would entitle them to a rock or two on the real Iguana Cay.

I looked around for Agent Forte. She was nowhere to be seen.

Kim, evidently not aware that Forte had gone AWOL, was already going ahead with her mission. She had sidled up to the projector and slipped in a different DVD, one of which I was particularly proud. Kim and I had stayed up all night working on it. We took each of the images from the Iguana Cay video and then showed how they had been constructed from various publicly available photographs—a beach scene from Kauai, a bungalow on Anguilla, wispy clouds from South Florida, and so on. We interspersed photographs of the real Iguana Cay, which I had taken just two days previously on our visit there. The climax of the little film was a shot of the lizards jostling for space in the sun.

Already the frantic atmosphere in Greenbacks had cooled, the looks of frenzied excitement replaced one by one with somber stares as parents grappled with the images appearing on the screen.

"Ladies and gentlemen, parents of Metropolitan, we have an announcement to make," Bronwyn repeated, louder this time.

Sunny gave her a strange look. Jeffrey was staring at our video. While all eyes were on Bronwyn, trying to understand what was taking place, Jeffrey lifted the black box and began to discreetly back away from the front table. Sunny wheeled around and saw him moving off. With a livid expression, she got up and marched after him. In spite of her limp, she was surprisingly swift.

When Jeffrey saw Sunny coming after him, he broke into a trot.

Heart racing, I headed after Sunny. Where was Forte? Out of the corner of my eye, I saw Dominique and Kim moving to block Jeffrey's escape. With the mothers in front of him and Sunny on his tail, Jeffrey dashed toward the pool in the center of the room. The mystified parents of Metropolitan were murmuring in confusion. All eyes were on Sunny as she rounded the island, tearing after Jeffrey.

By the time Sunny caught up with him, the parents were in an uproar, baffled and angry. Sunny threw herself at Jeffrey, knocking him into the knee-deep pool with a great splash. The box flew out of his hands and landed with a thud on the sandy tropical island. Sunny stumbled over him, then picked up the box and got up out of the sand. But just before she could get off the island, her feet seemed to get stuck.

The sand man had saved us, I suddenly realized. Out of sheer spite, he had sent quicksand after all.

I was right behind Sunny. As I rushed toward her, I saw Amy out of the corner of my eye. She was getting up, as though preparing to leave. Her wineglass remained in front of her. I gave it a good whack as I sped by, showering her upholstery dress.

Sunny staggered through the mire, her feet sinking deeper with each step as she struggled to make it out the back of the restaurant. I could see she was tottering. With a last burst of strength, I flung myself at her. "Don't even think about it!" I yelled. I hit her broadside and took her down. She landed with a great *squish*.

The box spilled out in front of us, its contents tumbling into the sludge.

As Sunny started to get up, her clothes and face splattered with the pasty sand, I saw her extricate one of her feet from the muck. She was about to try for another escape when I saw a blurred shape fly through the air in front of me. It was Kim, tackling Sunny and pinning her down. Jeffrey had gotten up by now and was diving into the muddy pile of spilled checks along with his assistant and Eve.

Two more blurred shapes flew in. Bronwyn knocked Eve to the ground. Dominique landed flat on top of Jeffrey. She straddled his chest and began slapping his face with both hands.

The cavernous hall was now filled with shouts and cries of outrage. The parents of Metropolitan had absorbed enough of the video, and they were scrambling through the sand and water to retrieve their checks and money orders, which had spilled out of the box.

"Everybody *freeze!*" said a woman with a loud, deep voice and a Kentucky accent.

I looked up to see Forte, legs splayed gangster-style. With one hand, she was brandishing a gun at the sprawling mudbath of parents. With the other, she reached into her breast pocket and pulled out a transmitter: "Backup! *Backup! Now!*" she ordered. Over on the big screen, my lizard scene was finally on.

"Where the hell have you been?" I asked Forte.

She looked at me reprovingly. "I gave you the signal that I needed to pee! I was in the bathroom!"

The parents slowly fell silent under the threat of her gun.

She looked around and harrumphed with satisfaction.

"I suppose it's alright now, anyhow," she said as the sound of sirens came in through the front door. She looked at the parents spread out around the floor and shook her head in disgust.

"I've heard city schools are bad," she announced in a loud voice, "but this really takes the cake!"

Chapter 19

Wake up, baby, day's a-breaking
Peas in the pot and a hoe-cake baking

"Jeffrey" had been right about one thing: Metro moms and dads were desperate to avoid a public scandal. They were also reluctant to pull their children out of a school they had fought so hard to get into. A week after the incident at Greenbacks, the rather shocked and subdued parent body gathered for an emergency meeting to discuss the school's future. As the principal owner of the school, Sally Smithson, aka "Sunny," was now in police custody, indicted for fraud and unable to post bail, and the school was the subject of quite a few claims and lawsuits. There was some doubt about whether Metropolitan had any future at all. On the other hand, the school did have some assets—namely, a prime chunk of Manhattan real estate, not to mention all the money it had scammed from the parents at the infamous auction.

Not surprisingly, it was Kim who saw through the mess to a

deal that would make everybody happy. Everybody except Sunny, that is, who was forced to while away her time in jail. "I propose that we all participate in a parental buyout of the school," Kim announced at the emergency meeting. "We make an offer to Sunny: In exchange for settling some of our personal claims against her, she agrees to turn over the school to us."

"Yes! We'll take over the school!" Bronwyn chimed in.

Eager to hold on to the brand name of Metropolitan and loathe to go looking for new preschools for their children in midyear, a large majority of the parents approved of the plan. It meant leaving most of their "donations" in the school coffers—but, then, many of the parents were too embarrassed to claim the money back. They appointed Kim and Bronwyn to lead the negotiations.

Sunny didn't have much of a choice in the matter. On a gray winter day, Kim, Bronwyn, and I paid her a visit on Riker's Island.

"How are the children?" Sunny asked, striving to maintain a pretense of concern as she spoke on the intercom through a thick glass pane.

"Our kids are none of your business," Bronwyn snapped.

Sunny shot her a look of disgust. "You are all so spoiled!" she said. "It's self-indulgent, narcissistic yuppies like you who have ruined New York City. You don't even know how privileged you are. You want to create the perfect child, the perfect reflection of yourself. Dressed in designer clothes and going to the 'best' pre-school. A little mini-me, as though the world needed more of you. You treat your kids like status symbols. And then you pay people like me to deal with the consequences! Why shouldn't I get my fair share?"

Without her jewelry and hair spray, she looked more like the hippie she had originally been.

"Look," Kim said, getting to the point, "you can spend the rest of your life in between jail and the lawyer's offices or—"

"Or you can turn over the keys to the school!" Bronwyn chirped.

Soon enough, the Metropolitan Preschool had reincorporated under new ownership. Kim and Bronwyn, who seemed to complement each other perfectly, were elected joint chairpersons of the new board of trustees. Under their leadership, the school immediately embarked on an ambitious program of reform.

The idea behind the reform program actually came from Anna. In the time she'd had off from school, after her "expulsion," I'd had some good, long talks with my daughter. She was now "four and one quarter," as she pointed out herself. For the first time in her short life so far, she and I seemed to speak not as parent to child, but person to person.

"Mommy, when I grow up, I want to be a teacher," she announced one day.

"Why, sweetie?"

"When I am a teacher, I will pay attention to all the children."

I realized that Anna's acting out at school had had a lot to do with Sunny's mismanagement. In her effort to hoard money and keep tight control over all aspects of school life, Sunny had understaffed everything, and had chosen inexperienced—and hence malleable—teachers. School life was so unstructured that it drove Anna batty. I dove into the research, checking up on the Italian philosophy that Sunny had touted, and came to a simple conclusion: Anna and children like her didn't need new educational philosophies—they needed more and better teachers.

With Kim and Bronwyn leading the charge, Metroplitan hired a new headmistress and supplemented Sunny's tenderfoot teaching staff with more seasoned educators. Recognizing that there was still a huge demand for elementary schools, the new board resolved to extend the curriculum up through the sixth grade. With the new endowment built up from the auction proceeds, they were also in a position to expand the scholarship program dramatically. They instituted a means-blind admission policy and created a generous financial aid program. Sunny's misbegotten auction, as it turns out, did what politicians had failed to do with the taxes—namely, create something like a viable public school.

As the new Metropolitan found its footing, Kim seemed to thrive in her quiet way. Her business seemed to be doing well—apparently, her duck-hunting skills had wowed a few important investors. Kim's husband, Eric, eventually got discharged from Bellevue and moved back in with the family. The adjustment wasn't easy at first, but soon Eric decided to cut the nanny's hours and take over Jake's care during the day. When I spotted them at school pickup or in the park, they both looked so happy. Eric was making up for lost time with his son.

But it was Bronwyn who truly flourished along with the new Metropolitan. She went around now in body-skimming dresses, her hair falling in loose waves around her shoulders. She oozed self-confidence. "Lloyd always freaked out if I didn't dress like a frigid housewife," she told me. "Now that he's gone, I feel like I can wear sexy clothes again!"

Getting rid of Lloyd had proved much easier than she had anticipated. Kim planted some spy software on Bronwyn's home computer, which collected so much evidence of his dates with "Randi" that he agreed to settle with her and move out immediately. "Now that his contact with his children is limited, he actually spends more quality time with them." Bronwyn flashed a sly smile. "Plus, when he takes the kids, I have my private yoga classes. From that instructor at Bloom. Remember him?"

Only Dominique still seemed to be twisting in the wind. She was still alone, and she was miserable. Whenever I saw her in those weeks after the auction, her face was puffy and her eyes red from crying. But now it wasn't because she was acting out some imaginary theater role. "I have been such an idiot!" she would say. "Alan is the love of my life. And he is gone. Now I have nothing. . . ."

One evening, Bronwyn, Kim, and I ran into Alan on the street, just as we were coming out from dinner. "She's miserable," Bronwyn told him. "She's desperate to have you back. She really loves you."

He crossed his arms over his chest. "If she loved me so much, why was it so easy for her to pack her bags and fly off to the Caribbean with some other guy?"

"She just got caught up in her own delusional thinking," I tried to explain. "Dominique is the kind of person who takes her fantasies a bit more seriously than—"

"I know she's like that," he said a bit hotly. "I knew who she was when I married her."

"So if you know who she is, can't you accept that she's capable of making a mistake?" Kim asked. "She really regrets it. And she has learned a hard lesson."

Alan exhaled. "She really hurt me. I guess I want to hurt her back."

I thought about the chaos of Alan's childhood and how it had propelled him toward a more stable existence. The shattering of that stability, the beautiful life he had made with Dominique, must have shaken him deeply.

"Well, when you're done hurting her, she'll be so happy to see you," I said. "I know for certain that she will never make the same mistake again."

Alan didn't say anything. He just nodded. But I could tell from his expression that he wanted her back just as much as she wanted him.

Chapter 20

Merrily, merrily, merrily, merrily
Life is but a dream

One evening not long after the auction, when I had a moment to myself, I took a long walk along the Hudson River. Instead of looking back on the city, I found myself gazing west, over the water, in the direction of the setting sun. I remembered when I was four years old, how my mother took me to the beach near the small town where I grew up. I remembered the sand falling through my fingers and the little sandcrabs scurrying out of my hands. I could hear the cries of gulls and pelicans, and I remembered chasing the waves out to sea and then running away from them again when they crashed ashore. Where was my mom? She was behind me, laughing. I wanted Anna to have a mother like that—relaxed and carefree, one who loved her as she was, not one who was concerned about building her résumé, one who could share with her the delights of nature. I knew it was time to move on.

* * *

"We're going to miss you so much," Bronwyn said with a wistful smile.

She sat down on our tattered sofa and rested her feet on one of the packing boxes.

While Kim, Bronwyn, and I discussed the plans for the new Metropolitan, Anna crawled around the boxes in our living space, with Richard ambling along behind her. In the past weeks, her fondness for her baby-cat-cow act had continued unabated. She had spent a lot of her time lying on the pillows, making gurgly noises. Anna's pediatrician and the therapist had repeatedly assured us that her regression was "just a phase" and that she'd snap out of it soon enough. Richard had decided to take it all in an optimistic spirit, and I was beginning to think he was right.

I knew that Kim and Bronwyn would improve things at Metropolitan, and it made me happy to hear them work on the details. Yet I was also filled with a sense of anticipation at the prospect of change. Metropolitan had been my testing ground. It had taught me how far—and how low—I could go. Kim and Bronwyn thrived in this terrain, and I knew that these women would remain my friends forever. But in my heart, I dreamed of something different.

We heard a knock on the door; it was Dominique, wearing a gunmetal-blue brocade jacket and matching wedge heels. "I don't understand why you are leaving us to go to Hollywood, of all places," Dominique said, greeting me with a kiss on both cheeks.

Her eyes shone happily, and she looked as beautiful as I had ever seen her. Ever since Alan had come home, she had been back to her old self. Perhaps a bit less histrionic, but she had recaptured her spirit and insouciance.

"Well, Richard's job offer is so good, we really can't turn it down," I said. In fact, I'd suggested to Richard that he apply for a tenure-track position at the University of California–Los Angeles. UCLA, as it happens, was also a powerhouse in seventeenth-century Dutch studies. My husband needed little persuading. "They've got some big guns in early astronomy!" he said, and flew out for an interview. They had offered him the job plus a hefty pay raise, and he had accepted.

He wasn't the only one with exciting developments to report. Thanks to Sunny and "Jeffrey," my own career had taken a surprising turn. I had found the experience investigating the Metropolitan scandals so intriguing that I had decided to change job tracks altogether. A series of talks with my new friend Agent Forte confirmed the decision. I was to become a private investigator.

First, I needed credentials. So I applied to the Los Angeles Police Academy. Initially, they had looked askance at such an untraditional candidate: older, a mother, with no prior interest or experience in law enforcement. But after Maxwell and Forte sent in glowing recommendations, they made an exception. I was in!

"Hollywood is full of fake people and empty promises. . . ." Dominique said now, taking a seat next to Bronwyn on the couch.

"That'll be good for business," I quipped.

"Does everybody want champagne?" said Kim, who had finally succeeded in opening the bottle. She started to fill up the flutes on the table.

"None for me," I said quickly.

"Are you sorry you ever flirted with Amy?" I demanded after our guests had left.

"Oh, come on, so Amy turned out to be a little needy," Richard said. He was busy packing up his things.

"Let's make sure to keep these alphabetized when we get to Los Angeles," he said as he grabbed a fistful of books from the shelves and stuffed them into cardboard boxes. "Last night I was looking for the German translation of Descartes and all I could find was the French original!"

"Okay, Mr. Sexy Professor," I said with a smile.

Richard closed the box and sat down next to me on the couch.

"Will you admit you went totally psycho over that class mother thing?"

"I never got *that* caught up," I said sheepishly.

"Yeah," Richard said, giving me a smile. "You were totally cool, calm, and collected. Especially, like, when you started breaking into other women's houses and hacking into their computers to find out who killed a hamster."

"Hey, a mom's gotta do what a mom's gotta do. Think of it as practice for my new career. Besides, you were the one taken in by your ex and her awful metaphors! Admit it! You were fooled! You liked the attention!"

"A little attention every now and then is not a bad thing," he said.

"You want attention?" I raised an eyebrow flirtatiously. "I'll give you attention." I started to reach for my husband.

"Waah," Anna interrupted us from her position on a stack of pillows on the floor.

We looked over at our daughter, still playing her baby game. "Kind of makes you wonder about number two, doesn't it?" Richard said.

"It's just a phase—even Dr. Dan says so," I said. I patted my belly. "But this time . . ."

"I know! I know!" He laughed. "You get to decide on the name! Call it Abelard if you want!"

I grabbed a pillow and pretended to aim for his head. He ducked, then grabbed me happily.

I looked at him knowingly.

"You don't really hate the way I toast bread?" I asked, pretending to be dreadfully hurt.

"Do you really think I don't understand people?" He smiled back.

We lay there for a while, not talking, just being together. *Like two palm trees on a sandbar,* I thought. But where was the third?

All of a sudden, we heard strange noises coming from the bathroom.

"Wuga-wuga-wuga." Anna must have sneaked away while we weren't looking, and she wasn't making her usual baby sounds. She seemed to be struggling with something. Richard and I got up together.

"Anna, are you alright?" I yelled.

"Wuga-wuga-wuga!"

Richard and I ran over to the bathroom and looked through the door.

There was Anna, sitting in the bathtub. Her intense expression was focused on a pair of stuffed animals between her legs: her orange-striped cat and a black-and-white cow. She was watching them carefully, as though expecting them to open their mouths and start speaking in rhymes. She glanced up at us, watching her from the doorway. She stared at us silently for a few moments, open-mouthed. Then she scooped up her two stuffed animals and, cradling them in her arms, stood up, carefully stepping out of the tub.

"This one is named Benny," she announced, pointing to the cow. "He is a he. The kitten is named Rosie. She is a she." She looked at us and blinked. "They are twins."

"Anna! You can walk!" I said.

Richard and I exchanged nervous glances. Would she get back down on the floor and demand to be carried?

But Anna looked at us with a quizzical expression.

"Of course I can walk," she said. "I am not a baby anymore. Benny and Rosie are my two babies. I am their mommy."

Just like that.

We stared at her wordlessly.

"Well, I guess that makes us grandparents," I finally said, glancing at Richard. He put his arm around my shoulder and squeezed me happily.

"I don't think she learned this at school," Richard said.

"No," I said. "She learned it all by herself."

He nodded and exhaled. "I guess that's how you learn the important stuff."

Then we gathered up Anna and her children, and all three generations moved back to our bed.